A.P BESWICK

Arnold Ethon And The War Of The Roses

Contents

Acknowledgments

This book is dedicated to my biggest fan, the one person who has always supported me no matter what. Mum thank you for everything you have ever done for me. Signed your fourth favorite child.

Chapter 1

Allon finished his fourty five minute commute in the relative comfort of his ice white Ford Focus. As he pulled up into the car-park, he looked into his rear-view mirror to see his dark, tired eyes staring back at him. It had been a long night with his five week old daughter keeping him and his wife aw for most of it. Colic was horrible and something that neither of them had experienced with the older children but Betty had been suffering with it and boy did he know it. The paternity leave had been great, spending quality time at home with his family. A rarity given the amount of shifts he had been pulling at work to save up for the various items they needed for the baby.

With the older three it had been easier. They had used the same pram that they had bought the first time around and with them all being boys they had passed hand-me-down clothes on to one another. Betty had not been planned and given that the boys were twelve, fifteen and seventeen, starting it all again at the age of fourty five was taking its toll on him. Of course, once the baby had been born any reservations about having another baby at their age had drifted away into the distance and replaced with the unequivocal love, that and tiredness.

Letting out a sigh he pressed the ignition button to bring his car to a sudden stop before running his hands down his face as he attempted to wake himself up some more. The dark purple patches underneath his eyes making him look like he had gone a few rounds with a boxer, something that he would much rather do right now than head into work.

Walking towards the towering entrance before him, Allon took comfort from the icy breeze that welcomed him. The crisp freshness of the air helped bring him around from the tired daze he found himself in. Before stepping in, he looked up at the one hundred and fifty-foot wall that surrounded his work. He felt every bit as awestruck at its size as he had on his first day there nearly fifteen years previously. He didn't love his job, but the pay was good, better than he would get anywhere else after-all, not too many people wanted to work in a maximum security prison.

The large rotating glass door was in front of him and Allon waited a few seconds before stepping into the opening and shuffling around to get through to the inside.

"Morning Al." A woman called, she was standing by a large body scanner that all employees starting and leaving work needed to walk through.

"Morning Ellen. How are you this morning?"

"I was about to ask you the same, but looking at those eyes, I am guessing the little one is still keeping you on your toes."

Allon put his rucksack into a tray as well as his car keys and wallet and sent them off across the rollers and through the smaller scanner. He stepped through the large body scanner which lit up green to show he was clear.

"Colic." He shrugged, the word itself sending a shiver down his spine.

"Oh jeez, had that with one of mine. You need to get some gripe water, that should help." Ellen said.

"Tried that, it hasn't worked." Allon waited for his tray to come through the rollers. "We will be fine in a week, it's just bloody hard at our age." Picking his rucksack up and throwing it over his shoulder before picking up his key and wallet.

"I hope for your sanity it passes soon Al." Ellen smiled as she waved a metal detector wand around him to check him over. "All clear Al, hope you have a good shift."

"Me too."

Feeling as though he was moving in slow motion today, he sluggishly walked across the room to the key rack. He placed his key card against the panel and a set of keys lit up and were magnetically unlocked. Allon removed them from their holster and clipped them to his belt. He was finally ready and headed to the large metal door to an airlock where a couple of his other colleagues were waiting to enter.

One by one, they all entered the corridor, shuffling through unenthusiastically. Once they were all through, Allon shut the door and locked it from the inside. It was an airlock so to get through the door at the other end, the first door needed to be secure.

Once through they all separated and Allon headed towards P wing, where he was based. Working in a maximum security prison was not the safest of places to be, but P wing was the worst of the lot. It housed the most dangerous criminals in the country, so dangerous that there were only seven inmates here. They spent most of their time locked in their cells up to twenty-three hours a day.

This job was not for everyone and they placed only the most experienced staff members on P wing. Those who had strong spirit beasts to support them if an issue was to arise. Now he had an extra family member his wife was pressuring Allon to change jobs or at least which wing he worked on. Allon tried in vain to reassure her that P wing was safer than the other wings because of the extra security in place.

Allon entered P wing and stepped straight into the office where he would receive his hand over and morning brief. Counting the heads, he could see he was the last one in. Allon sat down quickly on the nearest chair, having already missed the beginning of the handover.

"Nice of you to join us," Sandra Vey said. Her tone short and dismissive.

"Sorry Mam, the baby"

"I don't care Pierce. Shift started at seven, not ten past." She didn't appear to be in the best of moods.

Johnson and Ali glanced around to smirk at Allon with Ali smacking the back of her hand sarcastically at the ticking off he had just received before turning back to the front.

"So Davis has rung in sick this morning so we are a man short so you know what that means." Vey said.

The room groaned loudly. They all knew exactly what this meant.

"Great." Johnson called out. "We will have to spend all day putting up with abuse and dirty protests then?" speaking with frustration.

"You are being paid, aren't you?" Vey called back, shooting him down.

When they were short in numbers, the inmates received no time out of their cells, making them even less pleasant than their already low standards.

"Ali, you're on obs with Pierce this morning." Vey continued as she began allocating tasks to the team.

She's done that on purpose Allon thought to himself cursing being late. Observations were the worst job for him today, given that he was already struggling with staying awake. The boredom inducing task involved sitting right outside the high-risk inmates' cells, keeping them under close observation. They had two inmates considered high risk Gregor Masterson and Davey Leather, both were in for murder.

Davey had a complete hatred for menials and a list of victims as long as his arm with him, having incredible aggression shown through his hyena spirit beast. One which he used to maim and kill his victims.

Gregor also had a dislike for menials, he was here after he had got jealous of his ex-girlfriends new partner. Viciously attacking him with a hammer the first chance he had.

Neither of them had behaved in their time here and were no nearer to being released because of this behavior. They were both deemed both high risk because as soon as eyes were off either of them, they would be up to something that they shouldn't. The constant observations had been in place for the last twenty weeks and there had been no further incidents from either of them in this time.

At the end of the handover, Allon and Ali headed to the cells were. Relieving a portly, balding man from night duties who he did not recognise. His tired, purple eyes made Allon look fresh as a daisy in comparison.

"Been no issues." The man said before leaving.

"Bloody agency!" Ali said as she took her position at the bottom of the long corridor. "They always leave a right mess for us to clean up."

"Perks of always being short staffed." Allon said.

"Well, they get paid enough don't they?!" Ali scoffed as she leant forward and brushed away the bed of biscuit crumbs that had formed a blanket over the chair.

Allon walked down the narrow corridor. There were four rooms on the left side and three on the right. The walls and ceiling were bright white, which gave it a cold look. His footsteps echoed eerily as he did his first checks of the day.

Checking in the rooms, all the inmates were still asleep, apart from the last one that he checked.

The man was sitting upright in a chair reading a book, his dark shaggy hair partly covering his face. He had been here for about six months now. His behavior had been perfect since he arrived, which caused confusion to why he was on this wing. Allon knew he was here for the murder of a retired Elder, giving him a lot of credit from the other inmates. That was a given seeing that pretty much everyone detained here the Chichen had captured and prosecuted.

"Morning Levent." Allon nodded towards him.

Levent looked up from his book and nodded back to him without uttering a word. A red light was blinking around his neck. A sign that the collar he was wearing to nullify his connection to the spirit world was in working order. All inmates received a collar as soon as they arrived, rendering them as menials straight away, no longer able to summon their spirit beasts or any form of energy.

"We are short today I am afraid, so no one will access any free time today." He didn't mind having this conversation with Levent, as he never kicked up a fuss. Levent liked to sit and read his books and stay out of trouble. He wasn't able to do too much, due to a leg injury from when he was captured.

Levent looked back down towards his book and continued to read as Allon made his way back to the top of the corridor.

"It's going to be a nightmare when the other's hear that we

are short." Allon sighed as he sat next to Ali, picking up the observation book to write the checks he had just made. "There's only Levent up."

"What?"

Allon paused, wondering what he had missed.

"Gregor is always up at the start of shift!" Ali cursed.

Allon could have kicked himself. How could he have been so stupid? The two of them bolted down the corridor and up to the thick metal door of Gregor's cell. Gregor had a routine which he stuck to everyday and he would not deviate, something that the entire staff team knew because of the violent behavior which was exhibited when he had deviated from this.

"GREGOR?!" Allon called. "GREGOR answer me." Allon called assertively.

All they could see was a raised thin blanket that was covering his body.

"GREGOR!" His adrenaline surging, Allon reached for the door and his keys.

"Wait! That's not protocol." Ali pulled the chord that was attached to her personal alarm and it rang out. The shrill sound startling Allon. Nothing could wake him up this morning, the alarm however had done it in an instance.

Allon stopped what he was doing and waited for a response before entering the cell, as he should have done. He checked through the cell door and could still see a large lump underneath the sheet; he focused on it for a few moments.

"Is he breathing?" Ali pressed.

"I can't tell."

They continued to wait for a response to the alarm. Normally they would hear the footsteps of their colleagues clattering against the floor as they responded at speed. All they could hear was the ringing of the alarm, which continued to echo loudly against the empty corridors.

"Dammit, where are they?" Allon looked back through the door to check on Gregor. Still nothing.

"They must be on their way."

Allon couldn't tell if Ali was trying to reassure him or herself. "I know we are on low numbers but their should be a response by now." He continued to switch his sight from the unmoving lump in the cell and the bottom of the corridor, hoping someone would arrive. Then, without thinking, he broke protocol as he reached for his keys. Finding the one he needed he inserted it hurriedly into the lock, his hand shaking as he turned the key.

"Al! What are you doing?!"

But before Ali could protest any further, Allon had unlocked the door and burst into the cell.

"GREGOR! This is your last chance." He stepped towards him slowly. *Surely the response won't be much longer.* "GREGOR!"

"No need to keep shouting." A voice hissed from underneath the blanket. Suddenly Gregor sprang up from underneath the sheet and threw his large, muscular frame at Allon, grabbing him by the throat.

Allon grabbed hold of his arm and attempted to prise it away from his trapped windpipe. He gasped and gulped, trying to drag in what air he could into his lungs.

"Gregor, no!" Ali drew her baton and struck Gregor's bald head as hard as she could, but it simply bounced off him. Gregor turned his head to face her and grinned maniacally. Loosening his grip, he let go of Allon, who dropped to the floor heavily, gasping for air and coughing. Gregor stepped towards Ali and struck out, sending her crashing against the cell wall with considerable force. Grabbing hold of her ankle, he threw her towards Allon like she was a rag doll that weighed nothing. Ali clattered into Allon and let out a loud groan before slipping into unconsciousness.

"Ali!" Allon called, concerned for her welfare. Allon had little choice. He knew he couldn't fight Gregor in this confined space. He pulled Ali out of the cell and dragged her towards the top of the corridor. *How could I have been so stupid* he thought to himself as he dragged his colleague, all the while breathing heavily.

He placed Ali to the side and looked towards the cell door as Gregor's hulking frame made its way out from his cell, barely fitting through the doorway. Allon waved his hands around and emitted a soft green glow as he summoned his spirit beast. He pushed his hands forwards while focusing on Gregor, who was making his way up the corridor towards him. As he focused a Rhino took form ahead of him and charged towards Gregor with surprising pace. The Rhino let out a low grumble as it smashed into Gregor, sending him catapulting backwards.

At this, the other cells banged loudly as the other inmates noticed the fight that was taking place in front of them. Gregor rolled to a stop and quickly got back to his feet and ran towards the Rhino that was continuing its charge towards him. He vaulted over the top of it, using the walls at the side of him to jump from one side to the other, and began sprinting at Allon.

Allon braced himself and pulled out his baton as he prepared to defend himself against the brute that had murder in his bulging, bloodshot eyes. In an instance he was at him and Allon drew his arm back to strike him with his baton. Gregor's size and momentum took Allon off his feet as he speared him to the floor. Gregor let out a roar as he beat down on Allon, slamming his clenched fists down onto him repeatedly like a rabid gorilla.

Allon could normally parry the odd blow, but most of them were connecting with his head and chest.

Allon could feel himself drifting away he had nothing in him to fight this monster off. He thought about his family and the realisation that he might not see them again as blow after blow continued to rain down on him. Each one making it more and more difficult to remain conscious.

He noticed a glow from behind Gregor and a strange distorted light, then the figure of another person who looked as though they had just walked through a solid wall.

Levent reached forward and pulled Gregor off Allon and threw him to the floor before grabbing hold of the back of his head and slamming it to the side against the wall. Gregor's head crunched with the impact and with a dull thud, he slumped to the floor.

Allon's vision was heavily blurred, he thought he saw the figure step back through the wall. He could hear the footsteps of his colleagues getting closer to them as he attempted to pick himself up from the floor. Gregor was unconscious on the floor beside him. Blood was slowly escaping from his head and pooling around them. Allon shook his head, his ears still ringing heavily from the blows that he had received, and he walked across to Levent's cell. *Surely not.* He looked through the hatch to see Levent calmly reading his book sat on the end of his bed.

"Did you?" Allon asked.

Levent looked up and smiled at Allon. "You can thank me another time." and he looked back down to continue reading.

Chapter 2

"Come on Otto, hurry up." Arnold called out the car window. Arnold sat in the passenger side of the black Ford Ka Everett's parents had bought her for passing her driving test.

"What is it that takes you boys so long to get ready." Everett smirked.

"Your one to talk." Arnold fired back quickly.

"He has a point." George said from the back seat. "I thought Otto was making his own way there?" she added.

"He is. He has his new bike that he wants to travel down on but he needs to give us his bags before we head off."

"This weekend is going to be sick." Marrok said beaming with excitement.

The four of them waited patiently for Otto to leave his house. He was always late, but even by his standards this was pushing it. They had been sitting outside for twenty minutes waiting for him.

"This is ridiculous. Arnold, why don't you just knock on for him?" Marrok asked.

Arnold didn't want to, given that he did not want to come face to face with Otto's Dad after everything that had happened with them. Following the events at the abandoned coal mine, they had stripped Mr Redburn of his role as mayor of Oswald.

He was lucky to avoid a jail term but the judge presiding over his case, sympathised with the unprecedented position he had been in. Arnold however, could never forgive him for what he had done to Otto and to Everett, with Everett losing her connection to her spirit beast forever.

"Use the dagger Everett, he will have no choice but to hurry then." Marrok suggested.

"No." Everett said sternly. "I promised Otto I would never make him do something he didn't want to do. He trusted me with that dagger and after what he has been through, I wouldn't do that to him. It is tempting though." She smirked.

"Did you just tell a joke?" Arnold teased.

Everett was referring to the blade that Otto had entrusted to her so that his ability to transform into a were-jaguar would not be abused again. More than anything, Otto needed to keep his unique connection with his spirit beast a secret and he had entrusted his friends to keep it.

"Ey up, he's here." Marrok pointed to the door.

Otto stepped out with a grin on his face and a large bag hanging off his broad shoulders. He had a tent in one of his hands. "I've been waiting for ages for you lot."

"Seriously!" Everett did not look impressed.

"What?" Otto responded. "Pre journey loo trip."

"What is it with you and toilets?" Everett sighed.

"It's his routine, it's where he does his best thinking." Arnold laughed.

"He knows me so well." Otto dropped the large bag from his shoulder before walking to the back of the car and tapped on the boot to get Everett to open it. There was a small clunk as Everett released the latch and Otto swung the boot open before wedging in his bag and tent into the compact boot space. He

13

closed it with a thud that shook the entire car and walked round the side to poke his head through the window on Everett's side.

"Close enough Otto?"

"Something smells amazing?" Otto stopped for a moment, realising how bizarre he sounded and gave his head a wobble. "Erm, I don't know where that came from. Right well, I'm jumping on my bike now. I don't want to get stuck behind you lot." He spun away quickly and hopped onto his bike before putting his helmet on and starting up the engine.

Arnold poked his head out the window. "See you at Gisburn." He called out. Gisburn forest was roughly an hour away and easily accessible now that they had modes of transport.

Everett started up the car and followed Otto as he set off down the road on his bike. "Weekend away camping with friends. What could possibly go wrong?"

"Let's not tempt fate, Everett." Arnold laughed as they set off on their journey.

"Road trip!" Marrok called out, excited at the prospect of getting away for the weekend.

The journey didn't seem to take too long, even with Everett's over cautious driving contradicting her bullish nature. Although, she had showed a flash of hot-headedness as she shouted at various points in the journey at other drivers and in one case a group of cyclists that were taking up far too much of the road for her liking.

The winding roads leading up to the forest were like something you would see on top gear with the picturesque landscape twisting and turning in between the hills and trees. Arnold couldn't help but wish that he had a bike like Otto to go down these roads on, something he really wanted to do. With all his time going into his training at the Chichen he knew he didn't have any spare to learn how to ride a bike as well. Or taking and passing the tests.

Arnold and the others had arrived at Gisburn forest, parking in an area densely populated by trees. The smell of the woodland was the first thing that Arnold noticed as he began unpacking the car to get his tent. The air felt fresh. Marrok grabbed his large tent, Arnold watched him struggle with the many parts. He felt happy with his decision to bring a pop-up tent. Unzipping the large circular bag, Arnold grabbed hold of the folded-up tent and removed it. The tent sprung out in every direction, as it bounced off the floor and Arnold reached out to grab it before the wind took hold of it. It rustled loudly as the wind inflated it like a windsock. Arnold pinned the corner with his foot while he rummaged through the bag to grab the tent pegs.

"It's fine guys, you all chill out." Marrok said whilst wrestling with his complex tent.

"Don't worry, we will." George responded equally sarcastically, her pink pop up tent showing Marrok how easy he could have had it.

"Well, you and Otto had to get an oversized tent." Arnold said.

"Speaking of Otto, where is he? He should have been here before us the way he set off ahead like that." Everett quizzed.

At that moment, the low rumble of Otto's jet-black motorcycle mumbled in the distance. The rumbling from his bike got louder and louder, the engine eventually cut off as Otto dismounted his fake Harley and he made his way across to the others at their base camp.

"Took your time buddy."

"Have you seen the roads round here Arnold?" A wide grin

on his face. "Pretty sweet that ride." Otto placed his bike helmet on the floor beside Arnold's newly pitched tent before climbing in and sitting next to Arnold.

Marrok stopped what he was doing and frowned at Otto in disbelief.

"What?" He answered dimly.

"Seriously Otto?! Get out of there and help me get this bloody tent up or you can sleep outside."

"Like a pet!" Otto snapped back shortly.

"Sorry, I didn't mean to." Marrok withdrew, instantly panicking at the offense he feared he had caused.

A grin shot across Otto's face and the relief in Marrok was plain to see as he regained the colour in his face.

"Relax, I'm just messing. I won't be anyone's pet ever again, not with Everett at the wheel. Aint that right Ev" After being controlled by his Dad, Otto had entrusted control of his spirit to Everett. He trusted her implicitly to never misuse this against him.

"I'm still getting used to carrying this thing around with me. You make an ok spirit beast Otto."

"Well, it's safe to say no one is going to hurt you again with me by your side." He smiled.

"When did you get so chivalrous?" Arnold nudged.

"Excuse me, I don't need protecting." She smiled, but there was a sadness in her eyes.

Otto laughed out loud. "You have a good point." Otto laughed at this. Everett was not someone you would mess with and he admired her for that.

Arnold climbed out of the tent and took in the view. Their camp was surrounded by large pine trees which must have been anything up to fifty feet tall, maybe even higher. The environment looked darker than it should because of the canopy the trees were creating with only the odd beam of light making it through to them, giving the impression it was closer to the evening than it was. Otto eventually climbed out from Arnold's tent too and reluctantly helped Marrok finish erecting their oversized temporary living space before the five of them collected their bags and placed them in their tents.

Before long, they had all headed through the woods and walked towards one of the most popular spots around here, Lake Gisburn. The sky was clear with only a single cloud in sight. Arnold felt looked vaguely like a pig which reminded him of Everett's lost boar.

After reaching the lake, Arnold headed towards the rickety looking jetty. "Anyone up for going for it?"

"I, go on then." Otto responded immediately.

"We will let you test the water first." Everett added.

"I'll give it a go." Marrok said.

"Right then, that settles it!" Otto laughed. "It's fair warm out here so the water will be warm, right?"

The girls sniggered to each other at Otto's naive comments before simultaneously looking towards the end of the jetty to encourage him to take the plunge.

Within a few minutes, Arnold, Otto and Marrok stood side by side like brothers in arms. The three boys had removed their shirts, the extensive training each of them had undergone showing in the way their six packs were forming.

"Hang on lads." Otto stopped the other two just before they were about to jump off. He grabbed hold of his shorts, grinning at the others.

"Otto, no!" Everett laughed, not prepared for Otto's action.

Otto lowered his shorts slowly, as though he were carrying

17

out the world's worst strip-tease, while laughing to himself. Under his shorts, he revealed the tightest pair of bright blue speedos, wrapped around him like clingfilm. The girls did not know where to look with Otto confidently displaying himself for all to see. Arnold and Marrok found it hilarious, and they set about laughing together.

Once they had gathered themselves, they waited for one of them to make the first move. Arnold was feeling brave and set off, the other two quickly joining him as they began sprinting at speed down the old jetty.

Arnold wondered whether the rickety frame could support the three of them being on there at once but was surprised by its sturdiness. The gentle breeze was refreshing against his skin as the warm sun shone down on them from above. Arnold felt determined to beat the other two and dug deep to maintain his speed and keep ahead of the others.

He reached the bottom of the jetty first and launched himself into the air as high as he could, the weightlessness felt exhilarating. Arnold surprised himself at how far he could propel himself and let out a scream of enjoyment. Arnold bombed into the water, a crater of mist and spray shot up around him. His breath, was took away instantly as he plunged beneath the surface, completely shocked at how cold the water was. Kicking frantically, he tried to swim back to the surface, but his legs were a dead weight and he flailed his arms weakly to swim back up. He didn't feel as though he was moving at all at first, but within a few moments he propelled himself up and took in a huge gulp of air. His lungs ached with the icy chill and he could feel his body trembling intensely already. He frantically looked around for Otto and Marrok but could not see them. He wondered where they were, but he soon spotted them stood at the end of the jetty pointing and laughing.

"It's so, so cold." His teeth chattering. "Why did you not jump?"

"Because we are not stupid." Otto howled.

"Everyone knows the lake is freezing. No matter what the weather." Marrok added.

Arnold continued to kick his arms and legs, focused on not sinking to the dark depths of the lake below. Who knew what creatures were down there. Looking at the embankment, he could see George and Everett slowly stepping into the lake and making their way towards him.

"Wow, that is cold." Everett said as the water quickly reached her waist.

Arnold couldn't believe his luck, that she was his girlfriend. He couldn't help but notice how beautiful she looked. The sun made her skin look even more perfect, as though she was shining. The sight of her moving towards him brought about him a warmth that he very much needed at that point and he continued to tread water as she approached. Everett reached out to George, who was by her side, and the two of them held hands as they braved the coldness of the water together. Both squealed in tandem as the water rose higher and higher until eventually the two of them were in deep enough to swim.

Marrok followed Everett and George's approach, as it had seemed to work for them. Otto continued to perch on the end of the jetty, unsure whether he was going to join the four of them.

Arnold had acclimatised to the temperature and saw an opportunity too good to miss. He concentrated and motioned his hands underneath the water giving off a soft glow. Within a moment, his eagle spirit beast appeared and let out a loud squawk as it shot up into the air, its noise echoing loudly. It continued to rise high before diving back down towards the ground at incredible speed by tucking its wings in tightly by its side. Arnold could see its feathers vibrating because of the air pressing against them. A detail only Arnold could see because of his enhanced eagle eye vision. His eagle spread open its large wings, revealing an impressive wingspan, and clattered into the back of Otto. Otto howled as he found himself catapulted into the lake. He splashed into the water like a large salmon trying to get upriver and the rest of the group laughed hysterically. Otto pulled himself up to the surface of the water and took in a sharp breath of air whilst frantically kicking his arms and legs as he adjusted to the low temperature of the lake.

The five of them continued to mess around in the lake for a good chunk of the afternoon before eventually deciding to get out and head back to camp. Once back, Marrok and Arnold headed straight to the fire pit they had made in the centre of camp to put together what they needed for a campfire. They both grabbed their t-shirts and put these back on before they made their way further into the woods.

"We will get some wood for the fire." Arnold said to the others. He looked at Everett as she stood with her towel draped over her as she dried herself off.

In the next moment, Otto appeared out of nowhere and place his towel around her as well.

"You're freezing, here have my towel." He rubbed his hands up and down Everett's arms as he tried to warm her up.

Everett, confused by Otto, stood awkwardly as he tried to help her. "It's ok Otto, I can warm myself up."

George sat on a log that they had dragged into the centre of camp and was watching the two of them with their awkward exchange. She had her towel wrapped around her tightly and her knees to her chest while she dried off.

Otto looked confused at his own behavior and where his need to help Everett came from. "I'm just going to get changed," He said, before hurriedly heading to his tent, zipping up the front and disappearing.

"That was odd." Arnold thought out loud, did Otto just hit on his girlfriend? He gave his head a wobble to disperse the ridiculous thought, Otto would not do that to him. "Come on, let's get some wood." He said to Marrok, who had not seemed to notice the exchange.

Before long, the two of them had returned with plenty of wood to get their fire started and Arnold left Marrok to it. He insisted on creating the fire 'the old-fashioned way' as he had put it, refusing to use lighters, matches or fluid to help get it going. Sensing an opportunity, Arnold took himself over to Everett who was sitting in front of his tent and leant in to give her a kiss. Something seemed off. Everett seemed cold towards him. She shuffled to the side to let him sit down beside her, but she seemed distant.

"Are you ok?"

"Sorry?"

"Are you ok? You seemed miles away then."

"I guess so. I'm just thinking about my boar. It's my spirit beast, Arnold. I know I said that I am fine, but I'm not. I'm really struggling." Everett's eyes sparkled as they welled up with tears.

"It will be ok, I'm here for you." Arnold said. In an attempt reassure her and tried to hug Everett, but she quickly pulled away from him.

"I don't need a hug!" She snapped, "I need to focus on how

21

to get my spirit beast back. George is researching if there's anything that she can do to help me. I'm sorry Arnold, but I just can't, not at the minute." Everett stood up and walked across to sit beside George. George wrapped her arms around her to give her a tight embrace. Everett rested her head on George's shoulder before George rested her head on top.

Arnold's heart sank. He did not know where that had come from, and he did not know where he stood with Everett. *Has she just broken things off with him? Had he done something wrong?*

There was a horrible knot in his stomach and he didn't know what to do. He knew Everett could be brash, direct and had no issues speaking her mind. Since they had been going out, he had seen softer side to her, an affectionate one. Everett wanted space, but did she need to be so cold with him?

The noise of a zip being released came from the side of Arnold. He turned his head and saw Otto emerge from his tent.

"She won't have meant it mate."

"You heard?"

"Kind of hard not to, not really walls these things are they."

Arnold nodded in agreement. "I don't know what to do."

"Just give her what she has asked for, some space. Everything will be fine, trust me."

Arnold couldn't believe that he was taking relationship advice from Otto, but what he was saying made sense.

"Just don't Arnold it." Otto smirked.

Arnold couldn't help but smile and he felt grateful for the support that his closest friend was offering him. "Are you ok?" he asked Otto.

"Yeah I will be, can just be hard." He said, taking a seat next to Arnold. "I keep going from being really happy about being back to normal, to feeling sad and almost empty. It's really weird to describe."

"You have been through a lot mate." Arnold reassured.

"We all have." Otto added. "I'll soon be back to myself just need to adapt to the changes in me I suppose. I have felt more normal since Everett has had my blade. I don't have to worry about being made to do something I don't want to."

"I will never let that happen to you again."

"I know, cheers buddy."

The five of them spent the evening around the fire, but the atmosphere felt more subdued than Arnold had expected going into this camping weekend.

Chapter 3

Arnold hadn't had the best night's sleep. He lay on top of his sleeping bag, staring up at the roof of his tent. He could hear all kinds of birds outside, but there was one that had got under his skin, the low hooting noise he recognised to be that of a wood pigeon. Its distinct hoo hooing noise not being too dissimilar of that you would expect from an owl.

He felt hot and bothered as he flailed around trying to get himself comfortable and to have an extra half an hour's sleep. The problem was, he had far too many thoughts whirling around his head about Everett and he couldn't switch off.

Everett had not shared his tent last night, which is what they had planned prior to setting off on the camping trip. She had slept in George's tent. Arnold didn't want to lose Everett, she meant the world to him. He understood she was clearly struggling a lot more than she was letting on after losing her spirit beast.

I just need some space Everett's words played over and over in Arnold's head as he continued to try and get comfortable. It had cut through him like a knife. Why did she need space from him to spend time with George? It wasn't so much what Everett had said; it was how she had said it, which had unnerved Arnold the most.

He sat up, stretching his arms out as far as he could. His back cracked in multiple places, followed by his neck as he clicked his head from side to side to relieve some tension. He unzipped his tent and poked his head out. He could see Marrok was already sitting by the campfire, staring into space..

"Morning." Marrok whispered, not wanting to wake anybody else up.

"What time is it?"

"Half seven." Marrok blearily looked at his watch.

"What time did you get up?"

"About an hour ago, I've always been an early bird."

They could hear a colossal bear like noise coming from Otto's tent where he was snoring so loudly it would definitely scare off any predators that may have been lurking in the forest.

"Last night was fun." Marrok smirked at Arnold, trying to make light of the atmosphere which had spoiled the camp.

"Sorry, I wasn't really in the mood. Still, today is a new day."

"That's the attitude to have buddy."

Arnold thought it best to give Everett the space she had requested and to play it cool. He hoped that he did a better job of it than he had done last night.

"What's for breakfast?" Arnold responded to the gurgling sound coming from his stomach. "I'm starving."

"I can't find the bag with food in. I think I saw a shop a few miles down the road if you fancy a bit of a morning trek. We could be back before everyone wakes up."

"I fancy a run to blow off some steam." Arnold said, a run was just what he needed to work off his frustration.

"Sweet, sounds like a plan." Marrok stood up and stretched to warm up.

Within a couple of minutes, they stood side by side, just

outside of the base camp. They both knew that this would be far more competitive than either of them had let on.

"Ready?"

"Go." Marrok called and the two of them set off at a quick pace.

Taking a deep breath, Arnold ran fast and hard, wanting to set the pace. He had been training harder than ever at the Chichen and this certainly showed in his ever improving athletic ability. Arnold could see the sun over the horizon and from the top of the valley, a layer of mist hovering over the vast landscape. Around him, he could hear the many birds that sat in the trees.

Today is going to be a good day he thought to himself. A run was just what he needed.

They arrived at the shop with Marrok getting there first, but only just. The two of them bent forward as they attempted to catch their breath.

"That was quick Arnold, you are getting faster."

"Still not fast enough still." Arnold said as he panted heavily.

The two of them waited for a few minutes outside. When their breathing was a little less erratic, they stepped through the glass front door of the convenience store to collect the supplies they needed for breakfast.

"Make sure you have it next time we come, or else." A large man stood at the side of the counter with his hand gripped tightly around the young shop assistant's arm in the store.

"I told you, she is not here, I don't know where it is." The girl trembled in fear, her left cheek glowing where she had been struck by the man.

The brute must have been at least six foot five. His bald head had a large protruding vein bulging at the side. He dressed smartly in a grey suit complete with black shirt, with the top button undone.

The bell rang as Arnold and Marrok entered the store and the attention of the man turned to them. Two smaller men that were with him appeared to be searching for something in the store, turned to look at them.

"Nothing to see here, I suggest you leave." The smallest of the three men began. He was also wearing a suit, but he didn't appear as smart as the large man.

"You should listen to my friend." The large brute followed up. His accent was foreign, Arnold was unsure where exactly where he was from.

Marrok raised his hands outwards as he tried a diplomatic approach. "Listen, we don't want any trouble, we just came to get some things from the shop."

"There won't be any trouble, providing you both turn around and leave. No questions." The smallest man responded said quickly.

"At least put the girl down." Arnold volleyed, not impressed with the way she was being manhandled.

"Excuse me?" The third man spoke out. He was well spoken and had a look of disbelief. "Is there a reason you are telling us what to do? This has nothing to do with you. You need to leave before you get hurt."

The large man and the smaller man began laughing at them. Arnold felt a surge of anger at their sheer arrogance, his fists tightly clenched.

"Ha, looks like we have upset him." The smallest man said. "What are you going to do?"

"Nothing, I just think you should put the girl down and let her leave with us."

The three men began laughing hysterically at Arnold's offer.

"Listen here. I have had enough now. We have a job to do and you are getting in the way. Gregor, why don't you show him what we do to people who don't listen to us." The well-spoken man said, showing who was in charge of the group.

The largest man let go of the girl and turned to face them, a sinister smile on his face.

"Arnold! you had to poke them, didn't you." Marrok shook his head as he braced himself for the fight that was about to ensue.

The brute charged at Arnold and lunged at him as he got close enough. Arnold stepped to the side quickly, allowing him to go flying past him and into the door behind him.

"Just let the girl go, we don't need to do this." Arnold asked again. "We don't want any trouble."

The smallest man stepped forward and took a swing at Marrok, who blocked the first punch, followed by the second one. Marrok grabbed hold of the man's jacket and swung him back towards the well-spoken man, who he fell on the floor in front of.

"Really Mikel! you 're going to get beat up by a kid." He reached down and pulled him up from the floor with ease before straightening his suit. "Right then, lets have at it."

The two of them went for Marrok, who blocked their blows as they both attempted to rain down blows on him.

Gregor, by this point, had turned and had his eyes fixed on Arnold. He walked towards him at a fast pace, his breathing heavy with rage. "Stupid boy, I'll show you." He swung a right hook at Arnold.

Arnold raised both arms to block the attack before stepping forward into Gregor's personal space, slamming his closed fists into his chest with as much force as he could muster. Gregor's eyes bulged at the strength of the blow, his breath instantly taken away.

Gregor stumbled backwards down the aisle, holding his chest. "How are you so strong?" He gathered himself and ran towards Arnold and swung another punch at him.

Arnold blocked this and repeated the same move again, slamming his fists into his chest even harder this time. He ran forward and threw himself through the air drop-kicking Gregor and sending him flying into a row of shelves.

Quickly jumping up, he ran across to help Marrok. He was doing ok against the two men, but his bloodied nose highlighted he wasn't able to defend all the blows. Arnold slammed his fist into the side of Mikel's head, he let out a squeal with the contact and fell to the floor.

"Sucker punch." The well-spoken man said. "That's low." He launched an elbow and caught Arnold in the ribs, knocking him back. He began launching a series of blows and kicks at Marrok, which all made contact. He moved with incredible speed and strength, he was clearly skilled. The two of them stood opposite the well-spoken man, waiting for his next move.

It didn't take long, he launched himself through the air, kicking Arnold in the chest, followed by Marrok, all in one swift movement. Marrok slammed against the door into the outside space.

Arnold picked himself up, but the man was on him and quickly rained down another blow. He picked him up by the scruff of the neck and pinning him up against the window. Arnold grimaced as he tried to prise the man's hand off him. He slammed his forearm down onto the man's arm multiple times before he eventually let go of him.

The other two men had got up from the floor, Arnold did not

like the odds of three against one. He knew what he wanted to do, but there was not enough space in the shop. He stepped backwards towards the open door as the three of them moved towards him.

"You ok Marrok?"

Marrok was picking himself up from the graveled floor, groaning loudly as he recovered from the last blow. "I'll be fine. Think we need to take this up a gear."

The two of them stepped further back to allow some space between them and the thugs. Both of them motioned their hands around as they channeled their auro's. Arnold's hands glowed and he could feel his spirit beast rising from deep within him, his eagle flying straight upwards into the air before displaying its large wings. Within a moment, there was a howl and a white wolf stood side by side with Marrok.

"This just got interesting." The well-spoken man grinned.

"Look up there!" Mikel pointed towards the Arnold's impressive eagle spirit beast. "That's an eagle, that means you are."

"Yes, he is the one they have been calling the eagle warrior. The one the Chichen allowed in before he was of age. I am a little disappointed you didn't put up a better fight." The well spoken man said.

"I'm not done yet." Arnold scowled as his eagle swooped down towards Gregor and grabbed him with his talons, sinking them into his shoulders.

He shrieked as the eagle carried him into the air before dropping him to the ground in a crumpled heap.

Marrok's white wolf was baring its teeth aggressively whilst growling towards Mikel and the other unknown man. Mikel waved his hands around, as they began to glow, the leader interrupted him.

"That's enough Mikel, I will deal with this."

"But Valin?"

"I said that's enough!" With this, Valin motioned his hands to summon his spirit beast. A strong glow emitted around him as he focused his auro followed by the large spectral frame of his spirit beast; a gorilla.

It let out a battle cry before it started beating its hands wildly on the floor as it appeared to pump itself up to intimidate its enemies. Its muscular frame looking every inch as powerful as the creature commanded. The wolf and the eagle headed towards the gorilla, with the wolf covering land as fast as the eagle covered the air. They both lunged for the beast, but it was too fast for them. It slammed its fists into the side of the wolf, grinding it into the ground. Using its momentum to spin to the side, it dodged the eagle's attack. Reaching out the gorilla grabbed one of the eagle's legs before pulling it back down towards the ground with incredible force.

The eagle flapped frantically as it tried to break free, but it was to no avail; the gorilla used its other hand to grab hold of the eagle's free leg. Struggling, the eagle continued to flap its wings, the gorilla's feet embedded into the ground as it was dragged. The gorilla pulled down on the eagle, slamming it into the ground before picking it up and slamming it down to the other side.

Arnold dropped to his knees, crumpled by the shared pain that his spirit beast was experiencing. He looked up at Valin and anger took over. He covered the ground in front of him quickly.

The gorilla let go of his eagle and shifted its focus to Arnold jumping towards him, tackling him to the ground. For a moment, Arnold and the gorilla stared deep into each other's eyes as it pinned him to the floor. The spirit beast did not intimidate Arnold, but he was in awe of its power. The gorilla raised its hands above its head, ready to pound Arnold into the ground and let out a roar.

Arnold attempted to struggle free, but it pinned him to the floor and he found himself unable to put up a defence. The gorilla looked up as if it had sensed something else.

From the trees, a ferocious beast sprinted out. Valin's eyes lit up at the creature before him. It was Otto; he had shifted into his were jaguar form. His muscular frame ran towards the gorilla.

Otto grabbed hold of the gorilla's arms from above its head. The two shook violently as each tried to get the upper hand. Otto dragged the gorilla's arms down towards its side, a slow grumble of aggression emitting from him. Quickly, Otto pushed his legs up and kicked Valin's gorilla backwards away from Arnold.

Otto maintained his focus whilst standing his ground, protecting the others.

Valin clapped slowly. "Magnificent, simply magnificent. What on earth are you?" He dusted his clothes off and straightened his tie before continuing. "She would be interested in you, that is for sure. Gregor, Mikel, get up. We are leaving. Until we meet next time, eagle warrior."

With this Valin walked across to the black BMW which sat on the far side of the road, climbing casually in to the back seat. Gregor and Mikel limped across to the car, with Mikel taking the wheel. The car screeched off down the road and just like that; they left.

Otto was still tense and was emitting a low grumbling noise

as he panted heavily, still ready for the fight that was no longer here.

"Cheers buddy." Arnold called, but Otto didn't acknowledge him.

He was still in his were jaguar form and he wasn't shifting back, something that he was still getting the hang of but had not fully mastered. He turned and growled at Arnold, who held his hands up to show he meant no harm, his eagle dissipating back into his body. Otto continued to act aggressively but remained rooted to the spot, jerking like he was fighting with his own thoughts.

"Otto, it's ok. Calm down." Everett's voice called out from behind them. She ran beside Arnold and raised the dagger while speaking. "Change back, you can change back."

Otto emitted a soft green glow around him before his form changed back into his usual self. He screamed as his body contorted and scrunched into the fetal position on the floor.

"It hurts so much. Is everyone ok? I didn't hurt anyone, did I?" Otto spoke slowly as he tried to talk through the pain.

George rushed to his side and wrapped her arms around his body to comfort him. "You're ok Otto, you were just struggling to shift back." She helped him to his feet.

The shift had taken its toll on him, but he seemed ok in himself.

"I'll be fine." He attempted to step away from George, but his legs buckled.

Everett shot past Arnold and quickly grabbed his other side to help him stay on his feet, getting to him just in time. "You need to rest and recover. What happened?"

"I don't know." Otto recalled. "One second I was in my tent, the next I was here fighting that guy's spirit beast."

"What happened Arnold?" Everett asked.

"They were helping me. Those men, they are not good people." A softly spoken welsh accent came from the shop door, she was trembling from the fight that had just happened.

Arnold walked across to help her sit on a bench which was beside the front door. "What were they doing here? Why were they threatening you?"

"They were looking for the lady that owns the shop. I told them she wasn't here, she rarely comes here. She has shops everywhere, she has a lot of businesses. I need to call her and let her know what's happened. Thank you so much for your help, but I don't think they will stop until they find her."

The girl headed back inside without saying another word and before any of the group could ask her any more questions. The door swinging shut behind her, hanging limply off the hinges.

"What now?" Arnold asked.

"We still haven't got the bits for breakfast. I'm bloody starving here." Otto grabbed hold of his stomach.

"Seriously?! All that has just happened and you are still thinking about food. All three of you could have got really hurt then." Everett scolded.

"I think between the three of us, we had it under control Everett. We know what we are doing. Someone needed help, and we helped them." Arnold said in a rather cock sure manner.

"Yeah that's what that looked like." Everett fired back. "You know Arnold, there is a fine line between confidence and arrogance. Check which side you are standing on."

"Whoah Ev, no need to go in like that. The girl needed help, we couldn't just leave her." Marrok protested while jumping to Arnold's defence.

Arnold didn't understand why Everett was being like this,

and he wasn't in the mood for an argument. "Look, I'm not looking for an argument. Why don't you guys take Otto back to camp. Me and Marrok will finish up here and get the bits we came for."

"Ok." Everett's said.

Everett and George helped Otto into the car before climbing in themselves and heading off back down the road, the gravel spitting up as the spinning wheels dragged it up.

"I'm sure she didn't mean it mate."

"Pretty sure she did. I don't know why she is being like that, though. Come on, let's head inside and see if we can grab what we came for."

And find out what those guys were up to. Arnold thought, he had questions he wanted to get answers to.

Chapter 4

It was late in the evening, the sunset leaving only partial lighting littered across the compacted streets. A black Mercedes pulled up outside the Grand Chichen before a well-dressed driver climbed out to open the rear door. A lady exited she was in her early fourties and wearing an emerald business dress along with a light cream cardigan. Her long, wavy black hair was left loose letting the mild breeze decide her style.

"Ma'am." The driver nodded as she excited.

"Thank you Leon." she responded, her accent soft and well spoken.

Leon had been her driver for the last three years and she trusted him with her life. He had saved it occasionally. A debt that she didn't think she could ever repay.

"Where do you want me to wait, maam?"

"Park in the usual spot Leon please, it shouldn't be too long of a meeting tonight." She made her way up the large stone steps of the Grand Chichen, the cold stone clunking with the sound of the heel of the shoe tapping against it. To either side of her were carvings of Elder spirit beasts, ones that had fallen protecting their ways since this very first Chichen had been built hundreds of years earlier.

Making it to the top of the steps, she headed to the large

circular door that stood at the entrance to the extravagant building. The door huge, standing at least twenty feet in height and width. However, this paled in comparison to the workmanship and craft that had gone into the carvings that decorated the wooden entrance. This being the Grand Chichen, it was only fitting that the door denoted the many Chichen that were spread across the country protecting their respective counties. The emblem that represented each Chichen pristinely etched into the woodwork with mastery before a lacker was washed over the top to protect the ancient wood.

As the lady approached the door, it rolled open to the side as if it was being pulled by a large rope that no one could see. Stepping into the hall, all that could be heard was the echo of her heels reverberating around the large entrance area.

"Mrs Stone." The receptionist acknowledged. "Everyone is here, they are all waiting for you."

"Good." She smiled. "There is a need to keep up appearances." She carried on her walk to where the others waited. Mrs Stone continued her approach through the various winding corridors they were well lit, but there was an eeriness in the Grand Chichen when walking the halls alone.

Sensing something behind her, she suddenly stopped in her tracks. She glanced over her right shoulder to see if someone was behind her, nothing but the portraits of former Elders and Grand Elders that lined the walls watching her. Mrs Stone could hear the muffled voices of her colleagues coming from the chamber of which she had been making her way towards for the last ten minutes. Getting closer to the doorway, the distorted voices became louder and clearer. She pressed her hand against the old oak door and eased it open with a gentle push.

The room fell silent instantly and everyone else in the room stood in front of their seats quickly and quietly out of respect for their highest ranking Elder.

The circular room was lined with wooden seats, each individually carved into the pedestals that they sat behind. Behind each chair were different shields from the different families that had taken that seat throughout the years.

"Elders, please take your seats." Mrs Stone said, her demeanor calm and reassuring.

Mrs Stone made her way through the chamber taking the largest seat to the right of her. She sat down and looked around the room, nodding to everyone to show she was ready to start their quarterly meeting.

"Shall we begin, everyone? Miss Green, would you like to update us all on the Oxfordshire region?"

"Yes Maam." Miss green stood up and nodded towards the Grand Elder. Her dark skin complimented by the orange business dress that she was wearing. "Overall, in the entire region, we have had two hundred and thirty captures for crimes committed in the last quarter, most of which were sentenced to community service. Only twenty-seven of those committed crimes were deemed serious enough to warrant a custodial sentence."

"Thank you, Miss Green. Am I right in thinking this is a decrease in the last quarter?"

"Yes maam."

"Brilliant, that is great to hear." Mrs Stone complimented, smiling to the Oxfordshire Elder.

"Mr Whittaker, how has Lancashire been? Has there been any more serious crimes or have you finally got it under control?" Her words were sharp and cold as ice, showing her displeasure towards Mr Whittaker.

Mr Whittaker stood calmly and ran his hands nervously through his blonde hair, ensuring that it remained slicked back. He raised his closed hand to his mouth and released a dry, nervous cough. "Maam." He stuttered, "We have had one hundred and eighty-seven captures relating to crime. Fifty-five captured were sentenced to a custodial sentence, and the rest were fines or community service. We found one hundred and five captured to be menials."

There was chatter around the room as each Elder began whispering to one another.

"Quite a high number of menials, Mr Whittaker. This is most unusual. Is this linked to Levent?" Mrs Stone asked calmly.

"There is a clear link. Some even citing Levent as their reasoning for the crimes they have committed. We have seen an increase in menials trying to gain black market artefacts." Mr Whittaker addressed the room over the continued whispers. Becoming frustrated at his colleagues ignorance, he coughed loudly to bring their attention, but this was to no avail.

"Elders! A voice called from two seats down." A portly man stood in his seat, looking equally frustrated. He was older than Mr Whittaker with short grey hair which was receding away from his forehead. "Mr Whittaker is addressing the chamber. May I suggest we show some decorum and allow him to continue to speak without disruption?" He sat back down in his seat, his cheeks reddened with anger.

Mrs Stone cut an unimpressed figure and glared at the Elder, who had interjected. "Thank you, Mr Jacobs. Mr Whittaker, if you would like to continue."

"Thank you maam." He looked over to his fellow Elder that had addressed the room. "Thank you, Mr Jacobs. I have had contact with Gklyceria. There was an incident where an inmate escaped from a cell and attacked two wardens. One was seriously injured, the other would have been much worse than expected." He paused momentarily before continuing. "The wardens would have most certainly been killed if not for Levent."

The room gasped

"Sympathiser! You were in business with him when he tried to open a gate to the spirit world!" A womans' voice called from a few seats away.

"Here here" some of the other Elders called loudly.

"That is simply untrue." Mr Whittaker professed, ruffled at the accusation. "I did not know about Levent's involvement when I agreed to open the coal mines with Mayor Redburn."

"Mr Whittaker, do not allow the other Elders distract you from what you were saying." Mrs Stone cut in.

"Sorry maam. As I was saying, an inmate had escaped and attacked two wardens. It appears Levent used his powers to phase through his cell and defeat the escaped prisoner before returning to his cell."

"Impossible." The room talked amongst themselves once more.

"Elders!" Mrs Stone bellowed, and the room fell silent once more. "Mr Whittaker, is this account to be true? Was he not wearing his collar?"

"Yes maam, he was. The collar does not affect him and had not dampened his powers."

"You know what this means, don't you?" She pressed.

"Yes maam, it is highly likely that they will release him later this year. He was sentenced for taking the life of an Elder, but he has saved the life of two Wardens which will significantly reduce the time he must serve."

The noise in the room erupted with the furor of his fellow Elders who broke out in unison to discuss their disgust at the news. Someone who had killed a retired Elder and Doyen would be considered for release. This continued for a couple of minutes before Mrs Stone interjected once more.

"This is true. This is a law passed down through the Chichen for over a thousand years. We can't change this law. As you all know, it is set in stone."

Five knocks banged against the old oak door that sealed the entrance to the chamber. It echoed through the room, bringing instant silence amongst the Elders. The door slowly opened, its hinges vibrating as it revealed who was standing on the other side. Valin walked in calmly, as if they had invited in him. He was however, a most unwelcome visitor. He was alone and did not appear to be phased by the company he was now keeping.

"This is preposterous." Mrs Stone called. "Take another step into this chamber and I will see that you are captured and thrown into Gklyceria for contempt of the Elder council."

"I could not have timed my entrance any better, could I? What with you talking about ancient laws cast in stone. The kind that have to be followed." Valin was smug and callous. His black pinstriped suit, and highly polished brogues showing he took great pride in his appearance.

"Speak another word." Mrs Stone started but was cut off by Valin.

"We have a right to be here. Allow us to speak. It's written in stone." Valin was thriving in the moment and enjoying every second of this.

"Nonsense." Mrs Stone spat.

"She has the three seals of the Calmecac!" Valin roared, his voice echoing around the room.

The chamber fell silent instantly. As though his words had cast a spell, sealing everyone's mouths shut.

"That's impossible, the seals are hidden." Mrs Stone's voice quivered with Valin's claim.

"Hidden now found." With this, Valin reached into the inside pocket of his suit and pulled out three large coins.

"Even with the seals, they are useless unless you have a blood link to the Calmecac." Mr Jacobs called out from his chair.

"Is this enough proof?" A woman's voice called from the doorway. Her shadow entered the room first, before a hooded figure followed. Raising her hands, she lowered her hood to reveal her long, black hair. Her vibrant green eyes began surveying the room. Her skin was pale and there was a softness to her skin, a kind smile decorating her youthful face. She placed her hand within her cloak and produced the stone seals that glowed as she activated her auro.

"Trick's it's all tricks. You 're no descendant of the Calmecac. They died out hundreds of years ago. You are a fraud."

Valin was furious with Mr Jacob's poisonous words and he quickly reached to his belt and pulled out a dagger and launched it across the room straight at him. The blade thudded into the chair next to his head, Mr Jacobs slumping back quietly into his chair in shock.

At once, all the Elders jumped from their seats, ready to Punish Valin for his actions.

Mrs Stone appeared perplexed; she raised her hand to bring the chamber to silence while she addressed the strangers. "It can't be, it simply can't be." She muttered. "Helen? Is it really you? It has been so many years but you haven't aged a day."

"It's Hershel's wife!" Mr Jocobs bellowed. "What dark magic

is this?"

"It would seem you do not age in the spirit world," Helen addressed him. "Being bound there had its perks, it would seem."

"Bound to the spirit world? This is nonsense, you are clearly just a relative." Mr Jacobs challenged, his plump cheeks reddening with anger.

"Bound to a world to protect us from you." A wry smile formed in the corner of her mouth, her soft expression quickly changing to a sharp one.

"Why would you need protection from us?" Mrs Stone pressed. "Helen, what happened?" Mrs Stone showed genuine concern for her former colleague's missing wife. "Hershel said you had left out of the blue."

"An action of a desperate man. Do you know what it is like to be torn away from your family? To be forced into exile? All because of something that is out of your control. Your laws no longer bind me and they will no longer bind others!" Her face now contorting with anger her red auro consumed her body in its entirety.

"This is a sacred chamber you may not summon your spirit beast in here, it is forbidden." Mr Green was furious as he challenged the contempt Helen was displaying.

A tremendous roar filled the chamber as a large black scaled beast took form in front of Helen. Its eyes glowed with the same redness of her auro as if flames danced inside them, matched by the same glow in Helen's eyes. It was much larger than regular spirit beasts and stood at least nine feet tall, its dark scales shimmering in the candlelight. The beast bore its razor-sharp teeth to the elder council as Helen grinned wildly behind her spirit beast.

Collective gasps filled the chamber as all eyes fixed on the rarest and most dangerous of all spirit beasts stood before them.

"A, a dragon!" Mr Jacobs called out again as a dark green auro surrounded him. "Regardless of tradition, we must not allow this beast to remain!" He scolded, trying to implore the others to summon their spirit beasts alongside him.

The dragon shot forward at incredible speed and climbed over the top to Mr Jacobs' chair. He yelped as the dragon drew face to face with him, its mouth large enough to take off his head in one bite should it wish. The other elders glowed collectively as they readied for the fight.

"I invoke the right of the flower war!" Helen screamed.

The Elder's stopped dead in her words.

"The flower war? But this hasn't been used for hundreds of years, not since."

The Chichen took control from the Calmecac and destroyed an entire bloodline?" Helen finished. "We don't have anywhere near the numbers that the Chichen does but with the flower war."

"Yes, yes, I know full well how the flower war works. We will choose a champion to take part in it." Mrs Stone cut a worried figure, the colour draining from her face. "The faction that the warrior belongs to."

"Takes control." Helen finished smiling at Mrs Stone. "Of the country." She walked towards the exit of the Chamber. "One month. In one month, the flower war will start and everything will be at stake. It's written in stone after all." Helen walked through the door with a swagger, her dragon dissipating back towards her and Valin quickly followed, closing the door behind them.

The room erupted into chaos no sooner had they excited with

a section of the Elders rushing around Mr Jacobs who still sat slumped in his chair, his face pale with fear.

"We can't go through with this." A deep voice called, "She needs capturing."

Mr Whittaker left the side of Mr Jacobs, frozen where he sat. "We can't. The laws protect her."

"Mr Whittaker is correct. We must act quickly. That means choosing our warrior that are going to represent the Chichen. As you are aware as the elders of this country, you cannot represent the Chichen in this battle. I'm sure you all have Doyen's within your own Chichen's that you recommend." Mrs Stone understood how quickly they needed to move if they were to be ready. "Your badges, pass me all of your badges."

The room shuffled as each elder within the room passed their badges to Mrs Stone, each containing the emblem of their Chichen.

Grabbing a hat that one elder had passed her, she placed all the badges inside. Once the hat was full, she mixed the badges together before pulling a badge out; she examined the badge before declaring. "The red rose of Lancashire." She called out to the chamber. "Mr Whittaker, you must choose the Doyen to represent us in the impending flower war. You have until the morning. By then I will need to know the name of who you are putting forward so we can begin their training. We simply cannot lose this."

Chapter 5

The shrill alarm pierced Arnold's ear drums like a bolt through the head and he shot bolt upright as he groggily noticed his surroundings. His room was filled with darkness, it was he that had set his alarm at this ungodly hour. No matter how long he had been doing this for now, his body could still not get used to waking up earlier. But he needed to get some training done at the Chichen before college.

He gave out a loud yawn before slapping his lips together and reaching for the glass of water that sat on his bed-side table. The water felt crisp against his bone-dry mouth and quenched his thirst as he took a huge gulp. Arnold slid out of his bed and staggered across his room towards his wardrobe to grab his clothes for training and for college.

He tucked his college clothes into his backpack before getting changed into his tracksuit pants and a sweatshirt; they clung to him tighter than six months ago, as he had become a lot more muscular. Arnold was sure to be quiet as he didn't want to disturb his mother and father, who were still fast asleep across the hall in their bedroom. Sneaking across his room he reached for his door, pulling it open ever so gently before stepping carefully down the stairs to keep noise to a minimum. The stairs were always the hardest obstacle. Every day Arnold would slowly tackle them, but no matter how hard he tried, they always creaked loudly as he failed at trying to be a ninja.

Hopping down the final two stairs, Arnold stepped into his black trainers that sat waiting for him at the front door before walking into the kitchen to grab a banana that he planned on eating as he made his way to the Chichen. Carefully unlocking the door, he waited for it to click so that he could pull the door open.

"I see your skills of sneaking around are as good as ever." The deep voice calling him from the top of the stairs.

"Sorry Dad, did I wake you?"

"No son, I often get up at five in the morning before a long day at work." He chuckled to himself. "I'm up now, so I guess I will get myself ready and head to work. Mr Whittaker contacted me last night. He wants me to head in early anyway for a briefing. Just wasn't expecting to be up this early."

"Sorry Dad, I need to get going though if I am going to get a good training session in before college." Arnold fully opened the door, ready to set off.

"Just make sure you don't burn yourself out."

"Will do." He stepped through the door before closing it shut.

It was quiet outside, peaceful and serene. There were no cars driving around and the air felt crisp and refreshing. Arnold took a moment to appreciate the calmness. It was dawn, with the sun already rising above the few clouds that decorated the sky. Arnold walked to the bottom of his drive before setting off on a brisk walk way towards the Chichen, one of his favorite places.

Just over five minutes later, he scaled the many stone steps on the way to the top of the Chichen. He stopped momentarily when he reached about halfway up looking at the many spirit beasts of Elders and Doyen's that were carved into the stone with a unique mastery. He continued this walk around until he reached the carving he was looking for, his grandfather's spirit beast. There it was, the Elk that he himself had witnessed his grandfather summoning nearly two years ago when he rescued him from Levent. The horns being the most prominent part of the carving.

Arnold visited this spot every morning on his way in to the Chichen. This morning however, there was something different. The stone carving of his grandfather's Elk had been decorated with a single red rose, laid in front of it like someone had been to pay their respects.

Arnold found his gaze fixed upon the blood red rose at the foot of his grandfather's elk, the brightness of the rose shining against the cold stone. Arnold knew that if his Mum or Dad had been across, they would have said something. Arnold was intrigued who would walk up and place a rose specifically here when there were no others.

Or are there?

The thought entered his head and he couldn't shake it. Curiosity getting the better of him, he made his way around to the far side of the Chichen. Until he reached the other end of where his Grandad's carving was.

It's around here somewhere, I'm sure of it.

He didn't need to look hard. No sooner had he turned the corner of the stone steps that surrounded the Chichen, his eyes were drawn to something a few meters ahead of him. Another blood red rose lay peacefully on its side in pristine condition. He didn't need to guess where it sat, but he walked across towards the rose anyway. As he reached the hippo that was etched into the step, he knew that this was the tribute to

Charles Gray, the Doyen that he had saved prior to being invited to join the Chichen. This was the catalyst for everything that had happened since becoming an eagle warrior, Otto being fused with his spirit beast, Everett losing hers. Worst of all for Arnold it lead to his Grandad dying, an event which tore a deep hole in his heart and something he didn't know if he would ever get over.

When he reached the rose, to his surprise, there was a small envelope placed underneath the spiked green stem of the rose. His curiosity getting the better of him, he crouched down and tenderly lifted the rose to remove the envelope underneath.

Opening the envelope delicately, he wondered who would have left this here. His Dad had said that Charles didn't really have any friends other than his grandfather in their later years. He peeled it open and pulled out the small piece of card that was placed inside.

Dear Charles,
Say hi to Betsy for me

Thinking nothing of this, he placed the card back inside and laid it where it had been left. Something caught his eye, another card lay at the far edge of the step. He knew straight away that it was placed with his grandfather's Elk, it must have blown away before he arrived. His heart rate spiked and he picked the pace up as he ventured towards the next card, eager to read what it said. When he reached it, he grabbed it as fast as he could and hurriedly opened it, tugging out the card that was inside, tearing it slightly with his carelessness.

Dear Albert
Gone and forgotten
How does it feel?

Arnold felt a rage build up inside him. Who and why would

someone leave such a tasteless note here. He placed the card in his pants pocket and made his way inside. His mind dancing with rushed thoughts on who might want to leave the card here and after five minutes, he had nothing. He had no clue as to why anyone would do this, and it infuriated him.

Gone and forgotten
How does it feel?

His Grandad may have been gone, but he certainly was not forgotten. The more he tried, the less he could shift these words out of his head. He needed to let off some steam now and headed inside to get some training done to see whether this would distract him. He would pick this up with his Dad when he arrived for his early morning briefing with Mr Whittaker.

Just over an hour later, Arnold panted heavily in the changing rooms, his sweatshirt dripping with sweat from his time training. His plan to let off some steam had worked, but it had not stopped him from thinking about the card. Arnold was just as confused now as he was an hour ago why this card had been left. He just needed to get dressed now and see his Dad to see what he thought. First though, he needed to grab a shower as he was absolutely covered in sweat and an equally repugnant musk.

He grabbed a quick shower before throwing on his dark denim jeans and a blue sweatshirt that was slightly creased from being in his rucksack. Arnold hadn't dried himself fully, meaning his t-shirt clung to him slightly as he put his trainers on. He crammed his training clothes into his rucksack and threw it over his shoulder before heading out of the changing room, ready for the next part of his day, college. Arnold rushed down the corridor and up the stairs behind the reception area to get to his Dad's office. Grace wasn't in yet, meaning the reception area seemed somewhat haunting, with only his rushed footsteps to keep him company.

Reaching his Dad's office, Arnold pushed the door handle down to find it was still locked. He heard the big oak door slide to the side at the entrance and shot back to see who it was.

"How was your training?" It was his Dad who had arrived early, like he had told Arnold he would earlier. "Need I ask?"

He was referring to Arnold still breathing heavily and perspiring through his t-shirt, which was now clinging to him tightly.

"Try not to overdo it, son. You are pushing yourself hard."

"Don't worry Dad, I feel great."

"It's my job to worry." Arthur shuffled some papers on his desk before sitting down and taking a sip of the steaming mug of tea that sat on the table.

"I found this note by Grandad's carving this morning," Arnold reached into his pocket and produced the crass note he had found before passing it to his Dad.

His Dad took the note and read it before placing it on the table. "Most likely a menial that's linked to Levent."

Arnold was surprised that his Dad didn't seem phased by the note, "Maybe I am just over thinking it."

"I will have a look at the CCTV later and see if there is anything on there. In the meantime, haven't you got college to be heading to." Arthur took a sip of his tea before beginning to read through some paperwork on his desk.

With this, Arnold left the office. He made his way down the corridor and into the main hall, where he could see Grace setting up her desk at reception for the day.

"Morning Grace."

"Good morning Arnold. I see you have been training again

this morning." She spoke gently.

"I need to make sure I am as strong as I can be."

"Don't put too much pressure on yourself Arnold, you don't have to save the world."

"I need to keep my friends and family safe." His response was direct.

Grace came from behind her desk and placed her wrinkled hands on his shoulders. "This is about the fight you had whilst you were away, isn't it?"

Arnold paused, "He was so powerful, Grace. The only reason we were not worse of is because of Otto turning up."

"What do you mean?"

Arnold stuttered as he tried to correct himself. There was a reason they did not want the Chichen to know about Otto's unique ability to spirit shift. "You know, I mean it meant there were more of us then to fight him off."

Valin, the name, had stuck in his head since the camping trip and no one he had spoken to at the Chichen had any idea who the man was.

The circular entrance door rolled to the side, shifting Arnold's attention from Grace. Mr Whittaker rushed into the main hall. He looked different however. His usually pristine appearance looked somewhat disheveled, as though he were wearing the clothes he had on the day before. Mr Whittaker's hair was unkempt and matted. His black pinstripe suit was missing his blazer, his Armani tie loosely fitted around his neck, and his shirt rolled up at the sleeves. The large purple bags under his eyes were a sign that Mr Whittaker had little sleep, if any.

"Grace, please gather the Doyen's in the central chamber." A tremor in his voice as he rushed straight past them without actively looking at either Arnold or Grace.

"Ok Mr Whittaker, and what time should I schedule the meeting for?"

"Immediately." Mr Whittaker snapped as he marched towards the elevator. His echoing voice amplifying his frustration.

Arnold could not help but wonder what had happened to Mr Whittaker and why he would call a sudden meeting first thing in the morning. But he was and Arnold was curious to find out.

Grace was already behind her desk and dialing through to Arthur and the other Doyens based here, politely asking them to make their way to the central chamber, as Mr Whittaker had instructed.

Arnold could hear two or three doors open and shut within a few seconds of the phone calls and hollow footsteps rattling down the highly polished floor. Arnold stepped off to follow.

"Doyen's only Arnold." Grace's gentle voice stopping Arnold in his tracks.

"I'm er." He stuttered, "I just need to get some things from my Dad's office."

Grace gave him a skeptical look, but turned back to her desk and filed some paperwork. "Well, if you are stupid enough to get caught, then that is on you." Grace muttered to herself as her back turned on Arnold.

Arnold walked up the stairs and towards his father's office before diverting down the corridor and towards the lift. He knew that the lift went directly to the central chamber, but he also knew that when the lift doors opened, he would be exposed as they would know that someone had come down in the lift.

The stairs he thought to himself as continued down the corridor until he reached them. He knew they would be accessible as they were the fire escape, so could never be locked under any circumstance. Reaching the brown wooden door, he pushed the cold metal bar down to force it open and followed the many winding steps as he descended to the central chamber that sat at the bottom of the Chichen. This was where Arnold had been through his initiation and where he was presented as the first eagle warrior this Chichen had had for over three hundred years.

Being careful not to be loud, he delicately glided down the stairs with agility and speed as he tried to get to the bottom quickly. He had lost count of how many flights of stairs he had descended, but what he knew was that he was not looking forward to the climb back up, given that he had already had a heavy training session half an hour ago.

Arnold finally reached the bottom and placed his hand against the icy wall in front of him, leaning over as he gathered his breath. He took a few gulps of air to steady his breathing and slowly opened the door in front of him, being careful not to make any unnecessary noise. He stepped through the slight opening he had created and tiptoed a few steps to conceal himself behind a pillar. It was times like this he appreciated his enhanced vision as the room was dimly lit with the torches around the large chamber. Arnold peered around from behind the pillar and could make out Mr Whittaker sat opposite the doyens. He didn't need to worry about being too far away to hear because the acoustics of the hall helped project everyone's voices.

"The flower war? That's not been invoked since before the Chichen took power over the country." A smartly dressed woman with long dark hair was addressing Mr Whittaker.

"Yes Rosamund. It has not been invoked for hundreds of years."

Rosamund Potsun was the youngest Doyen at the Chichen,

but she was driven and intelligent. She was dedicated to her work, but remained grounded in her approach. She had joined this Chichen six months ago, but Arnold didn't really know her that well as she remained out of the office and in the field most of the time. He had overheard his Dad speaking to her in his office about keeping on top of her paperwork a few times, something that she didn't appear to prioritise.

"How though? I thought the Almec, and the Calmecac were no more." Rosumund's expression was that of concern.

"We have known about the Almec movements for sometime but these have remained quiet and they have kept themselves to themselves. There has been nothing to concern the Chichen about them." Arthur explained to Rosamund. "The Calmecac however."

Mr Whittaker cut in. "The Calmecac were wiped out in the great war, when the Chichen rose to power over them. Until last night, the Calmecac were deemed extinct."

"What happened last night?" Kobe asked. His large hulking frame filled his chair, making the others look small in comparison. Kobe had dark skin, a bald head and an average height. He was obviously strong, but his greatest asset was that he was a great listener. He was perfect to take council from, and Arnold knew his Dad respected him more than anybody in the Chichen.

Mr Whittaker withdrew into himself, looking uncomfortable with the conversation. "There are tons of people that we now know are involved. Valin is the first."

Arnold froze, recognising the name instantly.

"Who?" Kobe asked, his deep voice booming through the central chamber like he was using a megaphone.

"The same Valin that Arnold had a run in with?" Arthur pressed.

"I think so. Yes, he had the three seals with him, and he could activate them." Mr Whittaker looked concerned.

"That means he has a direct blood link to the Calmecac, right?" Rosamund questioned.

"This is correct. Not only does he have a direct blood link to the Calmecac, he is incredibly powerful. Given that he must have beaten each of the guardians entrusted to protect the seals." Mr Whittaker continued. "He has invoked the flower war. This means that the Chichen, Almec and Calmecac need to choose three warriors each to lead us into this war. As you know, this is to keep casualties to a minimal and ensure that the public remains safe throughout this. We don't want a bloodbath. The flower war prevents this by each faction choosing their best warrior to take part in the war. The winning faction will take power over the country."

"There is more," Mr Whittaker, looking even more uncomfortable, struggled to bring his eyes to meet Arthur's. "A second person invoked the right of the flower war. Mrs Stone has confirmed her identity."

"Who is it?" Arthur pressed.

"Your mother Arthur, she challenged the council."

"I see." Arthur took the information well and did not appear phased by it.

Arnold's heart began racing when he heard his Grandma was back. He already had a run in with her dragon spirit beast in the spirit world, an experience that wasn't pleasant. *It was her that left the letters and the roses.* The thought popped into Arnold's head. *That means that she is here.* Arnold did not trust her motivations but was surprised at how well his Dad had taken the news.

"Our Chichen has been drawn, hasn't it?" Kobe's deep voice

56

bellowed through the chamber once more.

Mr Whittaker nodded reluctantly, his face gaunt with worry. "I had to choose the strongest one of us from the Lancashire region. I had no choice."

"I'll do it, sir." Kobe stepped forward. "I understand the dangers that will present at the flower war."

"It's a death sentence." Rosamund cut in sharply. "It keeps the casualties to a minimum, but those chosen to represent do not come out of this well."

"I had no choice Rosamund. Our county was drawn. I had to pick the strongest of us. Arthur, you must understand."

Arthur was sitting silently in his chair, his face worn with the conversation he knew what was being asked of him.

"Arthur has a family sir?" Kobe protested "Please pick me, I will bring honour to the flower war for us."

"I have already put him forward. We need to win this war, otherwise we will lose everything."

Arthur stood up from his chair. "I understand, sir. I will do my best. If I may leave so that I can tell Eve and Arnold." He didn't wait for a reply from Mr Whittaker and headed towards the lift to leave the chamber.

Arnold's heart sank into his stomach. He had only just learned of the flower war and his Grandma returning, but knew that his Dad was going to be fighting with it. He now knew he may not return. This was something he couldn't bring himself to think about. He needed to get out and get to his Dad. His heart was racing, and he felt like he couldn't breathe. His skin became clammy and his thoughts were whirling around his head, thick and fast. The room spun. Feeling disorientated and hot, Arnold pushed back through the door and scaled the steps. With each step, he felt his legs getting heavier and heavier as he trudged his way to the top of the Chichen, his limbs feeling as though they were made from lead. The steps felt as they were never ending and the air continued to grow thinner and thinner as Arnold tried to press forwards; he needed to escape. By the time he reached the door, he felt as though his head was wrapped in bubble wrap. Everything around him, appeared to move in slow motion. He slammed his hands onto the refreshingly cold bar on the door and opened it.

The noise startled his Dad, who was walking away from the lift and back down the corridor. His face drew a look of confused concern for Arnold as he stood panting.

"Arnold?" Arthur rushed to help him.

The blood had drained from Arnold's face and as his Dad reached him, a strange sensation came over him as if he was vibrating intensely. Everything around him began moving at such speed Arnold could not make out his surroundings. When it stopped, Arnold crashed down to the floor with a thud. Placing his hands on the floor to gather himself, a sickening wave of nausea came over him, one that Arnold didn't think he could hold back. Taking a deep breath of air to quench the need to vomit, he felt different; the air felt different. It felt thicker, like a fog, an unnatural haze around him. Pushing himself up from the floor, he wobbled slightly from the disorientation.

He soon realised, that his Dad was no longer beside him. He was still in the Chichen, but nobody else was around. His Dad had simply vanished from in front of him. As fast as he realised Arnold's heart raced once more and he could feel his body trembling again. His surroundings began vibrating until he could no longer make them out. In the next instant, he found himself in the arms of someone, the sickening wave of nausea hitting him once more.

"Arnold!? What!? Where did you go!?" Arthur had grabbed Arnold to prevent him from falling and was holding him upright.

"What just happened?" Arnold stuttered. At least, that was what he was trying to say.

His Dad looked perplexed. "You vanished Arnold. For a few seconds you disappeared, then just like that you came back.""

Chapter 6

"People don't just disappear." Arnold was sitting in his Dad's office with a glass of cold water held in both hands, a minor tremor still within his body from whatever had just happened to him.

"You did." Arthur took a sip from the coffee that sat in front of him, his mustache raising slightly as he wrapped his lips around the cup. "I know what I saw."

"Did anyone else see?"

"No one else was around, just me. The other Doyen's and Mr Whittaker are still in the central chamber. I think it's best we don't share what just happened. You know what the council can be like. There's enough going on with the flower war and-." Arthur stopped, realising he had said too much already. "You already know, don't you? Where you down there? You are just like your Grandad, you know."

Arnold nodded. "I heard it all, Dad. That's when I ran back upstairs and felt funny."

"You looked like you were having a panic attack, but that explains why if you had snook down stairs. It will be ok Arnold, everything will be ok." His Dad tried to reassure him, although it appeared he was reassuring himself.

"Will it though?" Arnold looked down at the water in his

hands, the top of which was rippling from his involuntary shaking. "I heard you all talking. I know how dangerous this, this flower war is. What about Mum? What about me? What about Grandma?"

"Do you understand the reasoning behind it, Arnold?" He picked up his coffee and took another sip. "It has been hundreds of years since the last flower war. That is how long the Chichen have run the country for. Throughout history, flower wars are triggered as a way for factions to be in charge of the country. Until yesterday, the Chichen thought the Calmecac no longer existed and the Almec are only a few in numbers. Before the flower wars there were so many casualties Arnold, innocent people caught up in the battle for power, hundreds of thousands of lives. Understanding this couldn't go on, the Chichen, Almec and Calmecac leaders agreed that this needed to stop and the flower war was born. Each faction choosing their best warriors to fight in the war, this started off as a hundred each, however through time, this has lowered again to reduce the casualties and create a level field. No one faction more powerful than the rest, regardless of size."

Arnold sat quietly, captivated by his Dad's words. The two of them sat silently for a moment. "So you are going to go because it means others will not get hurt?"

"Exactly son, It's is my duty, I am a Doyen, my job is to protect people from harm. It doesn't matter what the cost is to me."

"But what if you die?"

"I will find peace knowing that others live." He replied calmly.

"What about Grandma? What do we do about her?" Arnold pressed.

"I don't know what to think about that. If she wanted to see me, she would be here. I'm guessing it is her that left the notes

61

outside. Triggering the flower war, would tell me she is hostile to the Chichen." His Dad took another sip of coffee and for a moment there was a blankness in his eyes as he become lost in his thoughts.

There was a broad knock at the door, the frame of which was instantly filled. It was Kobe. "Arthur, I don't know what to say. I have tried offering to take your place. Mr Whittaker won't have it."

"It's ok Kobe, I appreciate the offer, but it is something I need to do." He stood up from his desk and walked across to Kobe before extending his hand to him.

The two shook hands, and Kobe left the room once more.

"You need to get yourself to college. I need to do some reading about what happened to you in the hallway." There was an assertiveness to his Dad's voice, Arnold knew he needed to do as he was being told.

"What if it happens again?"

"I don't know Arnold. But we know who is the only person we have seen disappear in front of us before."

"Levent!?" The name instantly brought anger to Arnold . He hated him. The man who had murdered his Grandad right in front of him. Arnold was the reason he was now locked up in a high security prison, having captured him in the mines when he tried to open a portal between here and the spirit world. Then it dawned on Arnold, "I went to the spirit world, didn't I? Just like he can." Arnold felt sick instantly. He didn't want to be anything like Levent.

"Possibly. I can't think of any other explanation off the top of my head, I need to go to the athenaeum to do some reading. But first I need to see your Mum and tell her about the flower war." He paused for a moment, his face showing the pain of how much this was going to hurt Arnold's Mum. "Do you need dropping at college?"

"It's ok, I'll make my own way. Could do with clearing my head." He left the office. "Everything will be ok won't it?".

"As well as it can be."

His Dad's response did not bring Arnold the reassurance that he had sought. The two of them left the office before making their way to the front door of the Chichen. The walk down the steps seemed to take forever with Arnold's legs feeling heavy and slow. There had been so much that had happened this morning and Arnold hadn't even made it to college yet. He walked with his Dad until he got in his car and set off home to see his Mum and Arnold began his walk to college.

The streets were nowhere near as calm as they had been this morning on his way to the Chichen. The roads were busy with car after car passing him, there were children on their way to school and others, like Arnold, on their way to college. Breathing in, the air was still crisp and refreshing. Arnold liked the cold snap the cooler mornings that autumn brought, but it was November, nature was readying itself for winter.

There were too many things whirling around Arnold's head. The notes that were left at Charles and his Grandad's mural, the flower war, his Grandma returning and Arnold potentially stepping into the spirit world. He wanted to get to college and speak to the others and see what their thoughts were. He pulled his phone out of his pocket to ring Everett, then remembering how cold she was being with him, he put it away and continued his walk at a brisk pace.

Within ten minutes he had reached the entrance to college, which was attached to his high school. He was enjoying college, he got to choose his subjects now and he had chosen his favourite subjects history and physical studies. Arnold was now a strong athletic build, given that he had been training at the Chichen for two years. He smiled to himself as gangly year nine pupils walked past him that reminding him of himself before he began training.

"What are you smiling to yourself for?" Otto slapped his hand on to Arnold's back. "You look creepy." Otto's other hand was occupied by a sandwich which he had been making his way through. Since having the ability to spirit shift, one thing that had become more noticeable to everyone was Otto's insatiable appetite. Much to Arnold's envy, Otto had an incredible metabolism, meaning it didn't matter how much he ate, his body would simply burn it off.

"What you on this morning?" Arnold asked, trying to figure out what was on the sandwich.

"Cheese and ham, second breakfasts are great. Just can't fill myself up." Otto's speech became muffled as he rammed the last bit of the sandwich into his mouth.

"Morning boys." George was walking into college with Everett shuffling next to her. Everett still wasn't quite herself, her arms were folded across the textbook, as if she was hugging it to her chest.

"Morning Everett." Otto said more flamboyant than usual. Like he was a little giddy to be around her.

"Erm, Ok." Everett stumbled on her response, taken a back at how Otto had greeted her.

Otto's cheeks instantly blushed. Arnold didn't know what to do, or how to interpret the way Otto was behaving.

Does he fancy her?

Either way, Arnold wasn't impressed and he could not hide his displeasure from his face despite his hardest efforts. "Everett, can I borrow you for a minute?"

"It will have to wait Arnold, I'll speak to you later." Everett's response was short and curt. She was forcing her words out.

Arnold couldn't understand why Everett was being so cold with him. He had done as she asked and had been giving her some space, but things were getting worse between them, not better. It had been two weeks now since the camping trip and since then he had only spoken to her in passing. Only a courteous hello or good morning. One thing he was sure of now was that he was not looking forward to later.

Everett and George continued their walk inside, with Arnold and Otto trailing behind them.

"What was that?" Arnold's attention quickly turning back to Otto.

"What?"

Arnold felt dumbfounded "The way you spoke to Everett, just then."

"No, no, no. I don't, I didn't mean." Otto began stuttering and stammering his words, clearly uncomfortable with the situation.

"Forget it!?" Unimpressed, Arnold stormed ahead. He didn't want to look at Otto, let alone go through what had happened this morning.

It hadn't been the best start to the day and Arnold hoped things would get better. Before long, he had made it inside and towards the sixth form common room. It was a world away from having to register in forms and Arnold preferred the more laid back environments.

Opening the wooden door he entered the common room to a wall of heat, the radiators had clearly been turned up and Arnold felt initially taken aback at the temperature that greeted him.

He chucked his bag onto a faded, padded chair near the door and removed his thin grey hooded jacket so he could tolerate the temperature.

Arnold looked around the common room and could see Everett and George sat on the far side and deep in conversation. Most likely about him, well at least that was what he thought. Otto wasn't in the room yet, but Marrok sat at a table just a littler further from Arnold.

Looking up, Marrok saw Arnold seeming a bit flustered. "Morning." He placed his book down on his table and removed his bag to allow Arnold to sit down next to him. Taking the opportunity, Arnold took up the offer and slumped in his chair before resting his hands on his arms on the table in front of him.

"What's happened, mate?"

Arnold spent the next fifteen minutes filling in Marrok on everything that had happened this morning, barely taking a breath so he could get everything off his chest.

The morning passed uneventfully and Arnold had a free session in the afternoon. Taking the opportunity, he went to the Chichen and found himself training with a new level of intensity. His frustration towards the blatant way Otto had been flirting with Everett, providing the right amount of motivation that he needed today.

Arnold had finished his training for the afternoon and was making his way back to the changing rooms when he saw his Dad unlocking the door to his office. He raised his hand towards him to wave, but something didn't seem right to him. Something about his Dad looked different. His colour seemed drained as he looked a ghostly white, his expression gaunt and exhausted.

Arthur moved towards Arnold and attempted to smile, but his face didn't move, his skin wet with sweat. He raised his hand to wave back, but as he did, he fell forward and collapsed to the floor, crashing unnaturally to the ground.

Horror overcame Arnold, and his heart raced. Everything around him felt as though it was moving in slow motion. His heart pounded so hard he could hear it beating in his chest. "Dad!" he called out at once. It echoed loudly through the reception area, causing Grace to look up from her desk and towards Arnold.

Arnold felt like he couldn't take in any air as his chest was beating so wildly as he covered ground quickly. Within a moment, he knew it had happened again. Arnold had phased through to the spirit world. He could tell by the unnatural haze that surrounded him. Arnold continued running forward, he couldn't stay here. He needed to get back to his Dad and help him. His frustration matching his worry, his thoughts focused on his Dad. The unnatural haze around him disappeared and he could hear the call of Grace shouting for help as she knelt down next to his Dad, who remained slumped on the floor.

His Dad didn't look conscious and Arnold's heart raced more, his head a thick fog with worry. The unnatural haze appeared around him again as his Dad and Grace vanished from in front of him.

What the?!

Arnold needed to get back to his Dad. He needed to help him. Just like that, the haze vanished again, and he was back stood beside Grace and his Dad. She was rolling his Dad onto his back.

"Thank goodness, you're here Arnold." Grace called. "I think he is having a heart attack."

"A heart attack!" The words seemed to leave his mouth muddled and in slow motion, he couldn't believe what he was seeing. His Dad lay on the ground unresponsive.

"Arnold, ARNOLD!" Grace called.

Arnold snapped back into the room.

"Get the defibrillator Arnold, it's in a bag behind my desk."

Arnold shook himself and ran off to Grace's desk. While he was running, the unnatural haze kept appearing and disappearing around him. The air getting thick, then normal, increased pressure around him one second, then gone the next.

Arnold found himself at Grace's desk, which kept appearing and disappearing in front of him. He grabbed hold of the defib and spun on his heels, sprinting back towards his Dad. He wished his Dad would simply come back around and tell them all he was ok and that he didn't want any fuss being made of him.

His Dad lay motionless as Kobe began compressions on his chest. He dropped the defib next to Grace, who opened the container and unpacked the contents. In between compressions, she pulled open Arthur's shirt and stuck the pads on him, one on his chest and one on his side. The defib began talking.

"Please step away"

The pack called out as monitored Arthur's vitals before it sent a jolt of power coursing around his body. Arthur's body jumped into the air from the shock before Kobe began compressions again.

Arnold felt useless as he stood watching everyone trying their hardest to save his Dad. He could feel his body shake again and his temperature rose. His throat felt dry and each time he swallowed, it felt as if he was swallowing glass. His heart racing once more.

Then it happened and it was just as bad as the first time Arnold had shifted through to the spirit world. Everything began spinning, his Dad, Grace and Kobe all spinning until they blurred into one. He couldn't make out his surroundings. The disorientation was unbearable, and Arnold felt like he was going to pass out if the spinning didn't stop soon.

He slammed into the floor, finding himself winded instantly. Arnold continued to force his eyes shut as he held back the violent wave of nausea again. He failed and despite his best efforts, he was sick.

"No, no, no!" panicking he jumped to his feet and checked the room. The strange haze made it difficult to breathe and Arnold felt light-headed as he gathered his breath and became acclimatised to his surroundings. He banged his hand against the wall to vent his frustration, but it didn't calm him.

"Dad!, Dad!" He just wanted to be with his Dad, to know he was ok but now he found himself stuck here. He waited, knowing that when this happened last time, it was only for a few moments before he shifted back from the spirit world. This didn't happen though. A moment turned to a minute, a minute to twenty, then an hour. He was still stuck here. Arnold had spent the entire hour pacing the corridor, waiting for the strange sensation to overcome him, but it hadn't. He couldn't stop thinking about his Dad and whether he was ok, he needed to be with him. He needed to know that he was ok.

Arnold couldn't centre himself, his thoughts jumping around his head. At last though, he felt it, the strange sensation. The pull drew him back, a knot in his stomach that made him feel like he was going to be sick.

He found himself slammed to the floor and he knew he was back where he wanted to be, but the halls were clear at the

Chichen. His Dad was not on the floor where he last saw him, but he knew where he would be. He climbed to his feet and set off to the hospital to get to his Dad.

Every part of him hoping that he was ok.

Chapter 7

The taxi ride to a&e felt like the longest of journeys as Arnold pulled up at the front of the hospital. He grabbed the change that was in his pocket and dropped it hurriedly into the taxi driver's hand before exiting the vehicle. He made his way through the entrance to the accident and emergency in a panicked state and saw that there was no line at the receptionist desk.

"My Dad? I think he is here. He was having a heart attack." He panted.

"Ok dear, try to keep calm. What's his name?" The receptionist smiled politely at Arnold, her glasses sitting at the end of her nose. She had frizzy black hair and was wearing her NHS issued blouse.

"Ethon, Arthur Ethon." Arnold addressed her, trying to steady his breathing.

The receptionist typed into her computer before raising her eyes to meet Arnold. "He's in Resus. Head through those doors over there. The team should be able to point you in his direction."

"Thanks." Arnold replied before heading through the heavy blue doors, frantically looking for anyone who could point him in the right direction. His sight scattered across the room as he looked for his Dad. A nurse's station sat just ahead of him, surrounded by different bays in the room with dark blue curtains drawn around them.

"Arnold? Where have you been?" Arnold's Mum cried as she flung her arms around his neck. Her face red and blotchy from the tears she had been shedding. "Kobe, he said you ran away when your Dad was having a heart attack."

"I can't explain Mum, not now. Where is he? Is he ok?" Arnold just wanted to see his Dad.

"He is stable, but he is poorly. They won't let us see him yet." His Mum slowly released her grip from him and held both his hands as she tried to update Arnold.

She guided Arnold to the waiting room, which was lined with wooden chairs covered in a red fabric.

Arnold lost track of time and he did not know how long he had been there for. Arnold sat staring at the floor, his foot shaking rapidly as his knee shook in anticipation of any form of news from the medical team. His Mum continuing to pace up and down the room, muttering to herself under her breath. As far as Arnold could tell, she was trying to re-assure herself. Judging by how fast she was pacing, her approach was not working.

"Mrs Ethon?" An older man walked in wearing a dark blue tunic, a stethoscope around his neck implying to Arnold that he was a doctor. His tone was calm and assured, everything that Arnold and his Mum were not.

"How's Arthur Doctor? Is he ok? Please tell me he is ok?"

"He is poorly, but he is stabilizing. As I am sure you have figured out, he has had a heart attack. Mrs Ethon, Arthur will need time to recover but we expect that he will make a full recovery. We have had to insert a stent to help with the collapsed valve that caused the heart attack."

A weight lifted off Arnold's shoulders. His Dad was alive. Poorly, but alive and expecting to make a full recovery. "Can we see him?" Arnold pressed anxiously. He just wanted to see his Dad.

"Of course, this way." The doctor led them to a side room where Arthur lay in bed asleep. "Try not to wake him, he needs his rest."

"Thank you so much Doctor." Arnold's Mum's eyes filling with tears as she spoke. She turned to face his Dad. "Oh, Arthur." She whispered "You terrified me." She moved to the chair next to the bed and sat down before placing her trembling hand on top of his.

Arthur's hand was black and blue, which Arnold assumed was from the various procedures the medical team had had to carry out. His face looked weary. The heart attack had aged his Dad in an instance. He was going to be ok though; Arnold reassured himself once more. His Dad's chest moved up and down slowly, his breathing laboured. Arnold pulled a chair up and sat on the other side of his Dad and took hold of his other hand. "I'm sorry Dad, he whispered." He could not fight the overwhelming feeling of guilt that sat deep in his stomach. "You needed me, you needed me and I couldn't control my abilities." A sense of new found determination came over him. "I am going to get control of them, no matter what it takes." Arnold knew exactly where he needed to go and who he needed to speak to. After all, there was only one other person he knew of that could travel to the spirit world.

Chapter 8

"You want to do what!?" Otto was leaning against the wall in Arnold's lock up. "Are you insane? We have only just captured him, now you want to spend time with him?" Unimpressed with Arnold's idea, Otto shook his head in disbelief at what he had told them.

"I agree with Otto, it's a pretty bad idea to see Levent, never mind how you are actually going to get to him." Marrok perched against the cabinet at the back of the lockup, an old book in his hands which he looked up from to address Arnold.

The door to the lockup was open, with a refreshing breeze airing the container, removing the slight musty smell that stuck to the walls from the age of the books and relics that were stored inside. It was a warm day and if the container was shut, it would soon become too claustrophobic to function, let alone think.

"I didn't say it was a good idea, did I." Arnold snapped, frustrated at the situation. "I don't know what is happening to me, I can't control it and I can't let that carry on." Arnold had been up most the night worrying about his Dad's health and the fact that when he needed him he kept phasing through to the spirit world. His biggest fear being that for a moment he didn't know whether he could get back and that terrified him. His face looked weary, purple bags forming under his eyes.

Every time he blinked, he felt like he needed to sleep. With everything going on at the minute, he simply couldn't and he felt exhausted. "We need a plan." He fixated on the bookcase they had arranged all his Grandad's books in, the thought of having to read through them right now felt like the heaviest of weights and Arnold didn't know if he would be able to. "We need to see if there is anything that can help in these books." Arnold was sure that his Grandad's books would come through for him. It was just a case of finding the information.

"Does the Chichen know?" Marrok pressed.

Otto walked to the bookcase "Know what?" he studied the bookcase intently before removing the smallest book he could find to read through. It's blue dusted cover didn't have a title of it implying that it may be another of Arnold's Grandad's journals.

"That I transported to the spirit world, that I am linked to it somehow. No, they can't know, I don't know if I tr" Arnold cut himself off before he finished his words, it dawned on him he didn't trust the Chichen as much as he had previously and didn't know how they would react should they find out what he was going through.

"You have a link to the spirit world." Came a voice from behind him.

The boy's attention instantly drew towards the entrance to the lockup where George and Everett stood. Everett looked uncomfortable being there, her hand planted into the black leather jacket that she was wearing, the breeze catching her hair and blowing it into her face. George was wearing her beanie and a long multi coloured jumper that came down to her knees, her boots scraped against the gravel floor as she drew to a stop.

"What is?" Otto asked.

George moved into the lockup and headed towards Arnold, where she outstretched her hand to pass him a textbook. "What you are experiencing is because of a link to the spirit world Arnold. It's unheard of," George continued, "a myth, a legend, an old wives' tale. You shouldn't be able to."

"How do you know?" He asked taking the book from George. He glanced at Everett, but as soon as she looked at him, he diverted his attention to the book in his hand. He studied its brown leather cover before opening it up.

"That's one of my Granny's books." Said George, " It basically tells a story about a shaman who could teleport hundreds of years ago. Thought you may want to read it, there's some stuff in there about triggers."

Arnold stared blankly at the pages in front of him before looking back at George. "George, I will not lie. My eyes sting when I blink. I am that tired. If you know anything that can help, can you just tell me?" He snapped.

"Oi!" Everett barked, "don't talk to her like that." Her reaction over the top for the situation.

"Come on guys, let's keep it calm." Otto stepped in, trying to play peacemaker. "Thank you." His gaze rested on Everett for long enough for him to realise other people might have noticed.

"It's ok Everett, it's just tiredness." George replied, "Sorry Arnold, I thought you would want to read it, but I am happy to paraphrase. Stress. It's basically triggered by stress and anxiety. That's what the journal says happened to the Shaman that could use this ability. You need to learn to keep your stress and anxiety down, which should prevent it from happening."

"That's easier said than done." Marrok added. "How is Arnold meant to manage his stress and anxiety with everything that has been going on lately?"

"I understand that, but it is really important that you learn to, and quickly." George continued, her expression drawn and concerning.

"What will happen if I don't?"

"You need to read the book, but if you don't reduce your stress levels, you may end up like the Shaman. You may end up stuck in the spirit world forever."

"No pressure then." Otto quipped, trying to remove some of the tension out of the room. He failed miserably.

"I'd suggest going home and trying to get some sleep. That might be a good start." Everett was looking out into the grounds around the lockup.

"Take this, it will help you." George removed a flask from her bag and passed it to Arnold. "Drink it when you get home and you will definitely sleep until tomorrow."

George had been spending more and more time at the shop she had inherited from her Granny, learning the craft that her Granny had mastered over her life. George was skilled enough to make an effective sleeping remedy, and Arnold appreciated she had done this for him.

"Thanks."

"You don't need to thank me."

Arnold knew he needed to pack up now and head home to get some rest. He was no use to anyone this tired, and he certainly wouldn't be any use if he ended up trapped in the spirit world.

"We will leave you to it and catch up tomorrow. Get some rest." George finished and joined Everett at the entrance to the lockup. Everett gave a slight wave to the group, and the two of them headed off.

A vibrating noise sounded and Arnold turned to the bookcase where he had placed his phone. It was ringing on silent.

Arnold's heart sank as he snatched the phone, worrying in case it was an update on his Dad. However, looking at his screen, it was the Chichen ringing him. He answered the phone tentatively. All he could think about at this moment was going home to bed.

"Hello Arnold? It's Grace. Please, could you call into the Chichen? Mr Whittaker wishes to speak to you."

Arnold sighed. He really didn't want to, but knew he would pass on his way home. "Sure Grace, I'm on my way." He hung up the phone and placed it in his jeans pocket. "I need to head to the Chichen. Mr Whittaker wants to see me."

"We'll finish up here." Marrok said. "See what he wants, then go home and sleep."

Otto nodded and passed Arnold the flask off George, which Arnold took and left to head over to the Chichen.

Arnold arrived at the steep steps of the Chichen fifteen minutes later. He entered the building and shuffled towards Mr Whittaker's office. This was his first time in the building since his Dad's heart attack. It felt weird seeing the building operational again when it was less than twenty-four hours ago where they rushed his Dad to hospital.

As he approached Mr Whittaker's office, the door opened and Kobe filled the frame with his hulking physique. He looked perplexed, as if he had just received bad news. He could not make eye contact with Arnold.

"Is everything ok?" Arnold asked, concerned about Kobe.

He nodded. "You need to speak with Mr Whittaker. I am going to visit your Dad." He spoke slowly, as if fighting frustration towards Arnold.

Arnold felt confused. Why would Kobe would be off with him? Did he think he had run away when he was trying to resuscitate his Dad?

Stepping through the gap that Kobe had left, Arnold could see Mr Whittaker sitting behind his desk, waiting for him.

"Please take a seat Ethon." He gestured to the chair on the opposite side of his desk.

Arnold removed the dark wood chair and sat down as directed, an air of nervousness overcoming him. The chair stuttered as he dragged it back.

"There is no positive way to say this Ethon, your Dad is not fit enough to represent the Chichen in the impending flower war."

Arnold's spirit lifted instantly. This was the best news he had all day. His Dad no longer had to go against the other factions. When his health had recovered, he could come back to work without the risk of his life being lost in the contest.

Why then was Mr Whittaker looking so worried, why was he sat opposite Arnold unable to make eye contact with him. Mr Whittaker was always cool as a cucumber, today however, he was not.

"A different warrior has to be selected to fight in your father's place." He started.

"Kobe, surely Kobe can fight. He wanted to fight in Dad's place anyway." Arnold began explaining hurriedly, trying to get his point across.

"That is why Kobe was here. He was offering once more to take your father's place. A most self-less act indeed." Mr Whittaker continued to look uncomfortable and began shuffling around in his chair. "Unfortunately, Kobe cannot take the place of your father as the rules of the great council will not allow it."

Arnold couldn't help but feel confused. Why would they not

allow Kobe to fight in the flower war? It made sense being a powerful Doyen. It was the logical decision to make. "Why not?"

"Because of blood." Mr Whittaker said, "As you know, the spirit world we draw our energy from is intricately linked to our blood. The Elder council selected your father to represent the Chichen. He now cannot fight and only someone with a blood connection can take his place."

The colour drained from Arnold's face.

"It's you Arnold, you have to fight in your father's place. I'm so sorry but there is no other choice."

Chapter 9

Arnold could barely remember the walk home. His mind felt numb over the bombshell that just been dropped on him. He fumbled in his pocket half-heartedly, searching for his key before removing it and unlocking his front door.

"Arnold?," his Mum called as she came out from the living room to greet him.

"Sorry I'm late. I had to call in at the Chichen. Mr Whittaker wanted to see me."

"No, absolutely not! I know full well what you are going to tell me. After the last two years, I don't entirely agree with you being there. There is absolutely no way I can stand by and watch you take your Dad's place in this stupid war." Barely giving Arnold a chance to walk in before she began her rant.

"How do you—?"

"I know how it is your Dad has spoken about these things with me. Since he had his heart attack I have been waiting for Mr Whittaker to speak to you." She followed up.

"Then why didn't you warn me?" Arnold pressed.

"Because I was hoping they would see sense. That the Chichen would not make a boy fight against adults."

"I am stronger than you give me credit for." Arnold said, feeling a little belittled by his Mum's words.

"I don't think you understand the danger that you will be in if you represent the Chichen."

"I know exactly what it means. But it doesn't look like I have much choice though do I. If I don't take part, we will have fewer warriors which will make it harder for us to win." Arnold finished.

"And I would rather have my son at the end of it all." His Mum fought back the tears that were welling in her eyes. "As would your Dad."

"I'm well aware of the risks, Mum. I am going to do everything I can. I need to fight in Dad's place and I will. I just need to train and be ready."

"Arnold, the others taking part are going to be stronger, they are years ahead of you in their training. You are going to be up against the strongest from the Almec and the Calmecac." By this time, his Mum's sniffles had become full-blown sobs, and she reached for Arnold and gave him the tightest hug she could.

"I'll be ok Mum, I am going to do this for Dad." He squeezed her back before pulling away. "I am going to head up. I need to be up early. Need to train harder than ever, I suppose." He headed upstairs, the weight on his shoulders making the walk to his room feel impossible.

Making his way into his room, he threw himself backwards onto his bed before letting out an enormous sigh.

The remedy

He had almost forgotten. Arnold sat back up and rummaged in his rucksack before removing the flask that George had given him. He removed the lid before smelling the concoction and immediately regretted it. It smelt foul. There was an earthy smell, but the wild garlic burned the back of his nose as soon as he breathed it in. Arnold could not help but gag violently and for a second. For a second he worried he may vomit from the pungent aroma.

Arnold knew what he needed to do, he took a deep breath before bringing the flask up to his mouth. He wretched again at the smell, and it stopped him from taking in the vile concoction.

Staring down at the flask, Arnold psyched himself up once more. This time, clasping his nose with his free hand, he brought the flask up to his mouth again and gulped down the thick sludge as fast as he could.

He felt a wretch build up, but fought it back as he pushed himself to finish what he had started. When he had drank the last, he pulled the flask away from his face before heaving again. Barely keeping George's remedy down.

The last time he had taken a remedy, it had soothed his pain and calmed his nerves. This time however, Arnold's heart raced. His chest burning, he began to panic. What had George given him? What had he taken? He recognised this feeling; it was the same as when his Dad had his heart attack. The walls closed in around him and sweat dripped down his face. Arnold closed his eyes tightly as the room spun wildly.

What if George got it wrong?

After all, George was relatively new to the Shaman role that she had taken on since her Granny's passing.

The spinning was getting worse, the room spinning faster and faster. The nausea becoming unbearable. Suddenly Arnold felt as though gravity took a hold of him, feeling an immense pressure push down against him into his bed. Had Arnold not had his eyes tightly shut, he could have sworn he had been pushed through the centre of his bed as he felt the pressure push him further down. As hard as he tried through, he could not open his eyes, it was as if they were now glued shut. The spinning, the pressure, the feeling of free falling it was becoming unbearable and Arnold didn't know how much more he could take.

Arnold felt himself smash into the ground as if he had fallen from a great height. The floor felt cold; a welcome relief as it cooled his raised temperature. He wanted to stay where he lay, embracing the reprieve from whatever it was he had just experienced.

Slowly opening his eyes, the was met with an unnatural haze around him. George's remedy hadn't only helped him sleep, it had forced him into the spirit world. As he came around, everything started to slowly stop spinning, although the nausea was not subsiding as quickly as he would have liked.

Arnold noticed something out of the corner of his eye and in an instant he knew he was not on his own in this place.

"Hello boy." Levent smiled.

Chapter 10

Arnold's jaw clenched tightly, his hatred for the man stood in front of him was unbearable. It pained him that he needed his help. Taking a deep breath, he attempted to put his feelings to one side, a task that was harder than Arnold had imagined.

They were both in the spirit world. George's remedy had worked. Arnold had been transported, the hazy world around him becoming more familiar with each time he arrived here.

They were not in a room which Arnold felt was strange. He had imagined that they would be face to face in either Arnold's bedroom or Levent's prison cell. They were in a field; the air was still and hazy. It was warmer here, something that Arnold had never noticed before. He realised this was the first time he had been here and not been in eagle form.

"Feels different, doesn't it?" Levent smiled.

Arnold, still holding back the urge to punch him, remained silent. He estimated that there was about two meters between them, ground he could easily make up if he needed to. He didn't trust Levent one bit and was still questioning himself why he had actually come.

"You can unclench your fists boy, there's not a lot you can do to me here" Levent was wearing plain grey jogging bottoms and an equally plain, grey jumper. It was his prison clothing issued to him with when he arrived at the high security prison where he was now detained. "You still don't understand whether you are here physically or spiritually, do you?"

Arnold thought about it for a second. The difference between now and when he had shifted into the spirit world at the Chichen was that he was awake then. His mind may have been in the spirit world even if his body wasn't. After all, George's remedy had its limitations.

"How are we together, then?" Arnold asked curiously.

"Like it or not, the two of us are linked. Like you, I am asleep and my subconscious mind has been brought here. Most likely because of something you have done, I presume." He looked towards the sun and closed his eyes as if embracing the warmth he could feel against his face.

It clicked with Arnold straight away, he just wished he had figured that out for himself. He hated the thought of being educated by Levent. "You said we are linked," Arnold started. "How so?"

"Come on boy, use your brain." He paused for a moment before he continued. "No? Nothing? I am your uncle. Blood links us. It means you can draw me here in my subconscious."

"How do you feel about that lack of control?" Arnold smirked.

"Your assuming that I am not in control?" Levent taunted. "You have drawn me to this place. That doesn't mean you are in control." He took a slow step towards Arnold, the dried grass crunching beneath his foot. "You have brought me here to see you for a reason. That would tell me you need something from me, yes?"

Arnold could feel his temper flaring once more as Levent picked him apart.

"You might want to get a grip of that temper, you remind me

of me," He began laughing to himself.

Arnold's frustrations were at boiling point and he didn't know how he was keeping control of himself. He would have loved nothing more than to strike out at Levent, but he wouldn't let him goad him.

"So Arnold, what is it you need from me? What is it that I can help you with?" His words crisp and clear.

Digging deep, Arnold began talking. "I think I am like you," he started. "I don't know how, but I keep shifting into the spirit world. I don't have any control over it and I am worried that I am going to get stuck here. I know you can come and go to the spirit world, so you must be able to control it."

"Interesting," Levent held his hands behind his back. "It must run in the family." His sarcasm was apparent. "Tell me, why should I help you?".

Arnold paused. He did not have an answer to this question. "This is stupid," he snapped. "I shouldn't have bothered coming to see you." He looked around him before realising he had no way of forcing himself awake and leaving this place.

"You don't know how to leave, do you?" Levent smirked.

Not wanting to show any weakness, Arnold remained quiet and stony faced.

Levent took another step forward towards Arnold. "Tell me, what were you feeling?"

Arnold felt puzzled by this question, "What do you mean?".

"This is like talking to an infant," Levent's frustration was spiking. "When you transported to the spirit world, what were you feeling?" He said.

"Anxious," he replied.

"Interesting." Levent responded, "and where did you end up? When you traveled through?"

"End up? I was in the same place at the Chichen, but everything around me was different."

"Hazy like here?" Levent asked.

"Yeah."

"Interesting," Levent mused. "It sounds like your ability to travel is slightly different to mine."

Arnold felt curious about this information but did not trust Levent. His eyes were fixed on him, his anger towards him not subsided, simply under control. "Meaning?"

"Meaning I can teleport anywhere, well now I can. At first, it would be random where I would appear, but over time, I learnt to control it. You, on the other hand, don't do that, you spirit walk."

"Spirit walk?" Arnold had never heard this term before.

"You can move between worlds but at the exact same place where you stand. You could be powerful with this ability. No doubt the Chichen will want to run tests on you."

"They don't know about it."

"Interesting." Levent stood still for a moment. "Until next time." Levent lunged forward and pushed Arnold backwards.

With a jolt Arnold saw darkness followed by his dimly lit bedroom, the feeling of falling startling him awake. Had it been a dream? Had he really just been having a conversation with Levent?

Spirit walk he thought to himself. At least he had a little more information on what was happening to him. The only problem now was he needed to learn to control it, and fast.

Chapter 11

"Spirit walking, that sounds so cool." Otto was tucking into his third bowl of cereal, having arrived at Arnold's house at eight o'clock in the morning to find out if the remedy had worked.

"I can tell you it isn't nice," Arnold responded whilst also eating his breakfast.

Arnold knew that Otto's appetite had increased incredibly since having the ability to spirit shift, but it amazed him that although Otto looked physically stronger with a thicker frame. He hadn't become overweight. The amount that he would eat at mealtimes was astonishing.

Picking up his cup of coffee, Arnold placed it to his lips and took a large slurp before placing it back down on the dining table.

Otto finished his latest offering of cereal and sat back in his chair before letting out an almighty belch and grinning.

"Where do you put it all?" Arnold asked. "You should be about twenty stone for all the food you are eating lately."

"Kaliska reckons it's my metabolism." Otto was referring to Marrok's Mum and leader of the Almec. Arnold had not seen Kaliska since the night that they had captured Levent, but he knew they were in frequent contact with Otto. After all, he was a deity to them and they had offered any support Otto needed.

Arnold's Mum walked into the room. She looked as though she was not sleeping well. Purple bags had formed under her puffy eyes and her cheeks look slightly blemished.

"Are you ok Mum?"

"I am fine sweetheart, just worrying about you and your Dad. Don't worry about me." She walked over to Arnold and gave him a kiss on the top of his head. "I am going to the hospital to see your Dad. He is feeling much better now. Still weak, mind you, he is going to need looking after for a while, while he recovers at home."

"I know Mum, I will help as much as I need to."

"I will help too, Mrs Ethon." Otto followed up.

"You two are far too nice for teenagers. You should be out messing around with your friends and chasing girls. Not needing to look after your Dad and training for this stupid contest." Mrs Ethon cut a frustrated figure.

"It's ok Mum, sometimes things are just out of our control." Arnold stood up and walked across to his Mum, giving her a hug. "Can you let Dad know I will be over later once I have finished my training?"

"Of course I can, please don't push yourself too hard Arnold." His Mum finished before heading out of the front door.

Arnold cleared the table before grabbing his training clothes and throwing them into his backpack.

"Are you heading across with me?" Arnold asked Otto.

"Nope, I'll catch up with you later. I am meeting the Almec today with Everett and Marrok. They have been looking at how to help Everett safely harness the power in my dagger."

Arnold couldn't help but feel a little jaded. He would love to be involved in helping with this. However, with how Everett had been acting around him. He knew that it probably wasn't the best idea for him to be there. He understood Everett needed to focus on being able to wield Otto's blade. Besides this, Arnold had his own training to get through in order to be ready for the flower war.

Arnold left and headed one way to the Chichen, with Otto heading the opposite way to meet Everett.

When Arnold arrived at the Chichen Mr Whittaker was standing in the reception area, waiting to greet him. He was wearing his training robes, something which Arnold had not seen since Mr Whittaker helped Otto and himself connect with their spirit beasts for the first time. The dark purple tunic had the crest of the Lancashire region embossed onto the right sleeve. A blood red rose, the symbol of the county. Mr Whittaker did not look impressed. His arms folded, a frown etched across his face.

"What time do you call this Ethon?"

"Sorry sir?"

"Can I stress the severity of the current situation? I need you here every day Ethon. We have so much we need to get through. You are going to be competing against some very powerful people that do not agree with the path that the Chichen follows. They will not follow our rules of combat." His words spoken articulately and sharply.

"What do you mean, sir? Not going to follow our rules?"

"Capture, not kill is our rule Ethon. They will not give a second thought about taking a life in this contest and the bylaws permit it. Your life is in danger in this war and I need to make sure that you are as well equipped as can be." He walked away and headed towards the training room. "Get dressed and meet me for your training."

Arnold got dressed as quickly as possible and headed across

to the training room. He pressed his finger against the entry pad and waited for the door to unlock before heading in.

In the middle of the room stood Kobe, Rosamund and Mr Whittaker, all in their training robes. From Kobe's hulking frame to Rosamund's athletic ability, and Mr Whittaker's powerfully built physique. Arnold instantly worried about what this training session would have in store for him.

"Line up Ethon." Mr Whittaker commanded. "We have two weeks before the flower war begins."

Arnold did as he was asked and moved to the centre of the room. Strangely enough, he felt a bit of a buzz around him. He really enjoyed training and although he knew this was going to be hard, he knew he would come out of it stronger.

"You have two weeks with us before the contest will start. It is not just about your combat training, you need to have tactical awareness and show leadership during this war. If you want to survive."

"Go easy on the kid sir." Rosamund said.

Mr Whittaker looked less than impressed, "Go easy, he needs to know what he is getting into in order to be prepared Rosamund," He said. "Defensive stance Mr Ethon. Let's see what you have got."

As Arnold was getting into stance, Mr Whittaker launched himself at Arnold, barely giving him any chance to think. Arnold instinctively held out an arm to block the first punch, but he was unprepared for the knee to his side that he received, knocking him to the floor.

"Do you think your enemies are going to wait for you to ready yourself? They will strike the first opportunity that they get. Again."

Arnold climbed up from the floor, Rosamund was on him in

92

an instant and began raining blows down on him. Rosamund's blows were not as powerful as Mr Whittaker's, but she was fast and Arnold was only just able to block her varying kicks and punches. Suddenly, he felt his arms pinned to his sides. Kobe had locked him in a bear hug and was squeezing him tightly. Rosamund did not let up, continuing with blows against Arnold's body whilst Kobe held him firmly in place.

Arnold could feel his chest getting tighter, he was becoming light-headed, to the point where Rosamund's blows became a dull thud against his body in the background.

Arnold snapped his head backwards, catching Kobe in the jaw. His grip lessened and Arnold wriggled down and through the gap this created. As Rosamund attempted to kick him, Arnold crossed his arms in an x shape to block her effort before parrying her leg back to the floor and using his momentum to push her backwards.

Arnold only had a moments reprieve before Mr Whittaker slammed into his side once more, knocking him back to the floor.

Arnold panted for his breath. The onslaught he had just faced was brutal, but he had a feeling that they were only just getting started with him.

"Get up Ethon." Mr Whittaker was pushing him hard.

Arnold jumped to his feet and looked at where the three of them stood, each at different points in the room. He noticed Kobe had a bust lip, which made Arnold feel he wasn't completely useless. He needed to process his thoughts quickly to predict how they were going to attack him this time.

Rosamund was fast. She was going to attack first, followed by Mr Whittaker with Kobe delivering the strongest, final blow at the end, when he was at his weakest.

93

Arnold prepared himself, he was right. Rosamund flew at him with pace, followed by Mr Whittaker. Both aiming blows simultaneously with Arnold quickly having to shift his stance time and time again. He raised his arms over his head to protect himself, a move which Mr Whittaker exploited straight away by punching him in the stomach.

There was a flash of light and Arnold was sent crashing against the far wall of the training room with incredible force.

One of them had summoned their spirit beast. Arnold opened his eyes and pulled himself up once more, determined to make it through this.

Standing opposite the others, he readied himself in a defensive stance once more. "Again!" he called out. They were only five minutes in. Arnold was going to have to endure far worse if he was going to survive and it was a challenge he felt able to step up to.

Chapter 12

The aching in Arnold's body was intense, tonights training with the others had taken its toll on him but it was a welcome distraction from everything that had been going on. It was dark out and an icy chill had taken to the winter air. Arnold sat at the cenotaph with his training clothes on, accompanied only by a thin hoody. He felt a faint warmness in his muscles from his training, but he still dithered as he waited for Everett to respond to him

His phone was clenched in his hand. He was unsure whether Everett would come and speak to him, but he knew either way he could not carry on like this. He needed to know where he stood. The roads were quiet, given the time. Arnold checked his phone again and saw it was eleven o'clock.

Maybe she's asleep Arnold thought to himself. *Maybe I should just leave it until the morning*

Arnold had put up a good effort against Mr Whitaker, Rosamund and Kobe. However he still felt critical of his efforts, given how distracted he was with his thoughts. His Dad had nearly died and was still in hospital. His own life was in danger having to represent the Chichen as their champion. Not only this, his Grandma was back and behind the flower war and Arnold had a new ability he needed to learn to control.

Everett was still being the coldest she had ever been with him. Following the sparring session, Arnold had decided he needed to focus on things that he had some control of. He had texted Everett and asked her to meet him at the cenotaph to talk. Regardless of the time, he just wanted to know if there was any chance of them sorting things out with one another.

From around the corner, Arnold could hear the muffled talking of Everett and Otto drawing closer. The two of them appeared from around the corner. A rare smile was decorating Everett's face dampened as she saw Arnold sat waiting for her. Both she and Otto were wearing training clothes, the two of them looking like they had been training hard this evening, too.

Otto's clothes were stretched and torn and Arnold presumed this was from him spirit shifting into his were-jaguar form. Even though Arnold could understand the two of them spending time together. After all they both needed to get used to their connection through the dagger. This didn't stop the jealous pang that he felt hit him in the chest and he couldn't help but feel dejected.

"I'll, erm, just leave you guys to it. Well done today, Ev." Otto nodded towards Arnold. "See you tomorrow mate." He headed off, leaving Everett and Arnold alone.

Everett only stood around a meter away from Arnold, yet to Arnold the distance felt far bigger. They had drifted apart as Everett continued to push him away, something Arnold was struggling with this as all he wanted to do was help her.

Everett's arms were folded in front of her, partly because of the cold, partly for comfort. She brought her hand to her face to brush her dark, frizzy hair behind her ear that had escaped from her bobble.

"How are you?" Arnold attempted to break the ice between

them, but this was the most awkward he had ever felt around her.

"Tired, it's been a tough day. Kaliska has been showing me how to use the blade." Everett didn't seem as cold with Arnold, which raised his hopes slightly.

"How is that going?" Arnold asked, not wanting to dive into conversation about their relationship too soon. For the moment, Arnold was enjoying the prospect of a normal conversation with her.

Everett walked closer to Arnold and sat on one of the stone steps at the cenotaph and looked across at the closed shops on the opposite side of the road, as if gathering her thoughts. She sighed and exhaled loudly. "Its been so hard Arnold, I cannot fully explain it, but I will try."

Arnold could hear Everett's breath shake as she fought back tears, "You really don't have to if you don't want to." Arnold explained, not wanting to put any pressure on her.

Everett shook her head before wiping the tears from her eyes with her hoody that was stretched over her hand. "I want to, I think I need to." She wiped her eyes once more before continuing. "My spirit beast is gone. There is no way that I can ever get her back and since that day I have felt empty inside. Like part of me is missing. We didn't have our connection for long, but to have her ripped away from me has been unbearable. I don't mean to be the way I am with you, but ever since I lost her I feel that I have changed, not just physically but my personality too."

"What do you mean?"

"I mean that since I lost my spirit beast, I don't feel as strong, confident, or assertive as I used to be. She gave me that power, that strength, but now that she has gone. I just feel this void there. It is like I am not the same person I was before all of this. Arnold, you meant the world to me before this." Everett turned to face Arnold. Her face streamed with tears that shined against her perfectly dark skin.

"Meant?" Arnold focused on the past tense Everett used, he knew what was coming and he felt a tight knot in his stomach, waiting for the words that he had been dreading.

"I am so sorry Arnold, but I just have got no control over this and I can't help how I feel. The feelings I had for you, they are gone. Like they have been stripped from me. I can't explain it, but I know I cannot force it. That isn't fair on me or you." Everett was clearly distressed by what she was telling Arnold, her body shaking as she continued to explain how she felt.

"Give me time Everett, I can show you what we had." Arnold felt desperate, not wanting to lose his girlfriend.

"You don't get it Arnold," Everett snapped, "It isn't that I have forgotten how I felt, it is just those feelings have gone."

Arnold wanted the ground to swallow him whole and he felt his eyes well with tears of his own. He hated seeing Everett this upset, but he respected her and would accept whatever it was she wanted to do. Even if this was the opposite of what he wanted.

"Everett, I don't know what to say, I just want to help you."

"You can't fix everything Arnold and I am sorry but you can't fix this, fix us." Everett turned away from Arnold before standing, "I am sorry, I really am, because I know what we had was great." She set off at pace down the street towards her house, leaving Arnold alone with his thoughts.

It was done. Their relationship was over. Despite the pain, Arnold knew deep down that it was what was best for them both. Even though Arnold expected this to happen, it didn't make it any easier for him to manage his feelings and he spent the next hour sat on the steps of the cenotaph deep in his own thoughts.

When he got home, he shuffled upstairs as quietly as he could, not wishing to wake his Mum. It was past midnight and Arnold was exhausted, both physically and mentally. He didn't even bother with getting undressed from the clothes he had trained in. He simply removed his hoody and fell into his bed. His pillow swallowed his head and despite so much going on in his life, he just wanted to rest. He had never felt so exhausted.

Chapter 13

"Welcome back" The grainy voice of Levent rang through Arnold's head as he opened his eyes.

Levent was close to Arnold and for a moment he readied himself as initially he thought Levent was in his bedroom with him.

"Wakey wakey Arnold." Levent continued to tease.

"Wh, what do you want?" Arnold stuttered, still coming around to the unnatural haze he stood in. "Are we in the spirit world?"

Surveying the surrounding area, it didn't take him long to realise that he was in the same surroundings he found himself last time he saw Levent. The air felt thicker here, heavier almost, and Arnold felt as if the surrounding gravity were more compressed. As if he consciously needed to stop himself from being pushed to the floor by it.

"What do you want?" Arnold spat. He wasn't in the mood to see Levent. *so much for resting* he thought to himself.

"You didn't think you were the only one who could drag someone to this place, did you?" Levent grinned as he sat on a rock. He was looking up at the sky and letting the sun beam down on his face. Embracing the warmth that it provided.

Arnold imagined what it must feel like to be locked away in a maximum security prison and hoped that Levent spent his day stuck in a cell with nothing to do.

"What do you want?" Arnold repeated, his frustration rising

"Now, now, is that any way to talk to your uncle? I merely wanted to spend time with my dear nephew. You know we are more alike than you would have ever thought." He continued to goad Arnold.

"I haven't got time for your games, Levent!" Arnold spat, his fists clenched tightly as if ready for a fight. "I am not in the mood for this."

Levent roared with laughter as if he gained enjoyment from Arnold's foul mood. Arnold's aggressive stance did not phase him in the slightest, he appeared to lavish in it in fact. "Don't you see Arnold? You do have all the time in the world."

Arnold felt confused. He could feel himself being drawn in by Levent, wanting to know what he meant by his last statement. His eyes widened as he listened with more intent than he had previously.

Levent stood up from the rock and moved to just a couple of meters from Arnold, placing both his hands behind his back as he spoke. "It is only our minds that are in this space Arnold. The time spent here in this space does not draw parallels to the world where our bodies lie. My dear boy, you could be in here for a long time should I wish it." He began laughing to himself once more, amused at his own thoughts.

Arnold could not bear to be stuck in this space with the man who had murdered his Grandad in cold blood. Although Arnold sensed an opportunity with the wisdom that he had just been given. Maybe he could use this space to his advantage with the flower war.

"You know she is back, don't you?" Arnold asked.

"Who is?" Levent stopped chuckling to himself.

"Grandma, she is back, and she has triggered the flower war."

The colour drained from Levent's face and in that moment Arnold knew he did not know of her being free from the spirit world. His body language changed as the arrogant swagger he possessed eroded right in front of Arnold.

"No, that can't be." Levent stuttered.

This was the first time Arnold had seen Levent display any emotion other than anger, he found it quite unsettling that his Grandma had induced this much fear into him.

Levent began pacing erratically whilst muttering to himself. His whole demeanor changed from the powerful foe that Arnold had become accustomed to.

"What is it?" Arnold asked. "Why is it you fear her so much?" As it stood, Arnold had only heard that she had instigated the flower war and, until now, had done nothing further.

"She is dangerous. Who do you think gave me this scar? I didn't do as I was told when I was a boy!" Levent scowled. "Imagine what she will do to the Chichen. The people who she blames for her being trapped in the spirit world!"

Arnold had always assumed the scar on Levent's face was from one of his Lions and not inflicted by his own mother. It shocked him that his Grandma had done this to him, especially when he was only a boy.

Levent continued to pace around frantically. It was as if everything he had ever planned was being recalculated in his head. "I have an offer for you Arnold."

"There's nothing you can offer me. There's nothing I want from you. I want you to suffer for what you have done to me, to my family."

"Don't you mean our family?" Levent corrected.

In a moment of anger, Arnold lunged forward at Levent, who jumped away from him before his blow could connect.

"Steady, I suggest you listen to what I have to say boy." Levent's tone shifted back to what Arnold had grown used to. "I can help you, you can help me, that is all I am suggesting. An exchange, nothing more, nothing less. You need help learning to control your new ability before you get trapped in the spirit world like I did for so many years. I know firsthand the madness that can become of someone trapped in this place, the pain of losing everything that you hold dear." There was a sadness in Levent's eyes that resonated with Arnold. Levent gathered himself with gritted teeth before continuing. "I hate the Chichen. They killed the woman I loved on the day we were to be married. All for that stupid chalice. After that, I vowed to get my revenge on them for what they had done to me. Second to that I vowed to get revenge on my dearest mother for all that she has put me through and those that had trapped her in the spirit world with me." Levent's voice cracked as he explained his turmoil.

"Why are you telling me all this?" Arnold had no choice to question his motives. After everything he had done, how could he ever trust him. The thought of Levent loving another seemed impossible, but Arnold felt himself drawn back to the anger he felt towards Levent after he murdered his Grandad. If that is how Levent is feeling, maybe there was a deeper motive all along. "What do you want from me?" Arnold followed up.

"There will come a time when you and I will need to fight side by side, when that happens, I want you to think of this moment and you will have your answer." Levent's response was as if he was gazing into the future. "Do we have a deal?" He reached out his hand to Arnold.

Weighing up the options, Arnold knew that unless he got a grip of his spirit walking ability, he would soon end up trapped here and no use to anyone. He reached out his hand to Levent and shook it, albeit tentatively. It was a deal he felt he needed to make. If he was to survive the flower war, he would need to learn how to control his ability. The flower war was a week away and he needed all the help he could get.

"You said that time moves slower in this place? Does that mean if I train here whilst my body rests, I can get stronger?" Arnold thought aloud, hoping for the answer he desired.

"In some ways," Levent explained, "Physically your body will not change, you cannot strengthen your muscles whilst you sleep. After all, it is only your mind that is here. That said, you can practice your skills here, that technically when you are awake you will remember them."

"Like muscle memory?" Arnold questioned, remembering the phrase his Dad had told him not so long ago during a training session.

"More mind memory. You will remember things, feelings, emotions. You will remember how to do things, something that can prove an advantage for yourself."

Arnold felt more upbeat. He could train intensely in the spirit world while his body rested from training during the day. "What about spirit walking, how are you going to teach me to do that whilst I sleep?"

"I will teach you how to focus your thoughts and channel your energy. Then when you are awake, should the need arise, you can put what I teach you into practice."

The opportunity seemed too good to be true, but Arnold hoped he could take full advantage of it. Not only so he could get control of spirit walking, but so he could also train for the flower war. He was going to be up against the strongest from the Almec and the Calmecac and this way he might at least stand a fighting chance.

"When can we start?" Arnold pressed, eager to train.

"There's no time like the present." Levent smiled.

Chapter 14

Arnold woke and initially wondered if what he had dreamt had really happened. Had he really found a dream state in the spirit world where time moved at a speed which allowed him to train?

Arnold had been training with Levent. He didn't know for how long, but it had felt like days, whilst in the real world only a few hours had passed. He looked at his clock and it was six o'clock. He was still wearing his training clothes from the night before. His body ached from his training at the Chichen, but he felt invigorated, like he had gained an advantage. He was tired, technically he hadn't stopped training. However, his body ached no more than it should have. What Levent had told him had rung true. Arnold lay in bed for another hour thinking about everything going on in his life. Everything was so much simpler before he had a spirit beast. For a moment, he wondered what it would be like to just have school to worry about. No flower war, no Valin, no were-jaguar for a best friend.

Would all this have happened if I had been a menial he thought to himself.

When it reached seven o'clock, Arnold grabbed a quick shower before heading downstairs. His Mum was already sitting at the breakfast table in her cosy pink dressing gown. She was staring blankly across the table, lost in her thoughts, her eyes purple from a lack of sleep.

"Are you ok Mum?" Arnold asked.

His words startled her and she jumped before bringing her gaze towards Arnold. "Sorry sweetheart, I was miles away there. You sit down, I'll fetch you some breakfast." She went to stand up, but Arnold stopped her.

"It's ok Mum I can sort myself, I'll make us a brew." Arnold shuffled off to the kitchen and made some toast and a cup of tea each before returning to the dining room.

For a moment they both simply sat at the table, no noise or conversation between them, just the ticking of the grandfather clock that stood in the corner.

Arnold took a bite of his toast and encouraged his Mum to do the same. She reluctantly obliged and began eating the jam on toast that Arnold had made her.

"We will be ok Mum, everything is going to be ok." Arnold reassured, he was alarmed at the toll everything was having on his Mum. If he could take it all away from her he would, she was a worrier at the best of times but between his Dad's heart attack and the flower war it was no wonder the effect it was having on her.

"I hope so, Arnold. The Doctor has said that your Dad might come home in a few days. Maybe he will know what to do about you and this flower war." She still didn't agree with Arnold going and would no doubt look to stop it from happening.

Arnold didn't feel as apprehensive about the impending war as he had the night before, now that he had a way to intensify his training. "I am going to survive this Mum, for you and for Dad." Determined to beat the odds that were stacked up against him. "I know you won't, but try to stop worrying about me. I need you to focus on Dad. That is going to help me focus on coming out of this alive."

"I will try Arnold. It just isn't easy. You 're too young for this, it is too much pressure for you to carry by yourself." His Mum reached out and grabbed hold of his hands. "I am so proud of you Arnold."

Arnold felt a lump in the back of his throat. He needed to be brave for her; he needed to survive this for her. Arnold squeezed her hands tightly, affectionately. "I am not by myself Mum, I have you and my friends behind me. That's all I need."

He stood up from the table and moved towards his Mum before wrapping his arms around her and giving her the biggest hug he could muster. In this moment, Arnold felt safe. The embrace made him feel like a child again and as much as he had hugged his Mum to make her feel better; he realised how much he had needed it too.

Two days later, Arnold found himself sat at the bottom of the stairs, his foot tapping almost uncontrollably with the anticipation of his Dad's return from hospital. His Mum had left two hours earlier to pick him up. The doctor said his Dad was well enough to return home to start the next phase of his recovery. For the last two nights Arnold had remained in the spirit world within the dreamscape that he and Levent had created. He had been training hard to learn to manage his spirit walking ability, but so far it had given him little reward for his efforts. During the day, Arnold would train just as hard at the Chichen. Normally he would rest today, but given that the flower war started in just a few days, Arnold knew there was no time to rest.

For now, he just wanted to enjoy the moment and spend some time with his Dad before heading back to the Chichen.

Arnold's heart jumped as he heard a noise at the door, but

this was just the postman doing his morning rounds. A letter dropped through the letterbox, however there was no stamp attached to it. On the front of the envelope read; Arthur Ethon. Arnold stared at it, initially believing it to be a card from a neighbour wishing him well. It didn't take long for him to recognise the handwriting; it was the same as the notes left at the Chichen by his Grandma.

Jumping up, Arnold grabbed hold of the handle and flung the door open before running to the bottom of his garden. There was no sign of anyone outside. Arnold looked over the envelope before surveying the street once more. His chest was pounding. He used his thumb to break the seal of the envelope and pulled out the card inside. It was a get well soon card, the image of a grey bear hugging a smaller bear. It was a mother and child. Arnold opened the card to read the message inside.

Dear Arthur,

Get well soon.

He knew in an instant that it was from his Grandma, but he was unsure whether he should give it to his Dad. After all, he needed to keep stress free following his heart attack. His attention was diverted by the sound of a car and his heart rate spiked once more as he saw his parent's traveling towards him. He folded the card and placed it into his back pocket. The car pulled up with his Dad sat in the passenger seat; he gave him a smile as Arnold approached the car door. Arnold pulled the door open, just wishing to be with his Dad again. The thought of nearly losing him still painful, but at least now he was home.

Arthur slowly excited the car, using the door to steady himself. He seemed out of breath just by doing this, although for a moment he appeared to be enjoying breathing in the fresh air. His face was gaunt and thinner than prior to having his heart attack. Stubble was forming on his face and Arnold swore his hair was greyer than it was before. It shocked Arnold, he was used to seeing his Dad command such a powerful frame. He now looked a shell of his former self.

Arthur looked over at Arnold and could see the worry etched across his face. "Come here," Arthur reached forward and pulled Arnold towards him.

Arnold was surprised at his Dad's strength and wrapped his arms around him as they hugged each other. It was an embrace he feared he would never feel again and he wished it would last forever. Being with his Dad again, Arnold felt safe.

Chapter 15

"Focus!" Levent barked at Arnold, the frustration apparent in his voice.

"I'm trying!" Arnold spat back.

Arnold sat in the tall grass in the field in the spirit world, his legs crossed, his eyes tightly shut. Breathing in the thick, unnatural air through his nose slowly and exhaling through his mouth as he had been instructed.

Levent stood with his arms behind his back, circling Arnold like a shark would circle its prey. His eyes fixed intently on Arnold as he continued to talk to him. "Open your mind." He growled.

"What does that even mean?" Arnold felt the force of a blow to the back of his head from Levent. He didn't like being talked back to, but Arnold couldn't help himself.

"Do you want to be stuck here?" Levent asked sharply, unimpressed with Arnold's cockiness.

Arnold had been trying, but he had gotten nowhere. He had learned nothing other than Levent wasn't the greatest of teachers, not that this surprised him. His commands were short and he couldn't hide his disappointment and frustration towards Arnold when he wasn't instantly able to do what he had commanded.

This didn't bother Arnold that much, all he wanted from Levent was to learn how to control his spirit walking. Arnold just hadn't imagined it being this hard to master compared to everything else he had studied and learned in the previous years.

Sitting cross-legged, Arnold felt in a calm state, his mind clear as he had been persistently directed. Forcing his eyes shut, he thought of his Grandad and for a split moment felt a semblance of shame for the fact he was now working with the man who had murdered him.

Jumping up from the ground, Arnold could feel his frustrations rising. "I've had enough. This is a waste of both of our time."

"Careful boy, you risk sounding like her." Levent scolded, unimpressed with Arnold's latest outburst.

"Don't!" Arnold barked, equally unimpressed with Levent's words.

"Or what? Admit it, you 're more like us than you think. Your grit, your determination to your cause," Levent posed for a moment before continuing, "Your anger." He finished, taking pleasure in purposely goading Arnold.

"Shut up!" Arnold spat, "I'm done with this" Turning from Levent, his fists clenched tightly, his knuckles whitening.

"You're done when I say so." Levent grabbed hold of Arnold's arm forcefully, applying pressure to assert his dominance.

This was not something Arnold was willing to put up with and his anger got the better of him. Spinning on his heels, he turned to come face to face with Levent and swung his free arm towards him quickly and sharply. Levent's eyes grew with rage and he raised his hand equally fast to catch Arnold's fist in his open palm. Levents' face contorted as he processed Arnold's insolence and he threw his head forward, making contact with Arnold's face.

Arnold saw stars and stumbled back. He was surprised by the throbbing feeling he felt across his face. Bringing his hand up to his nose, he realised he was bleeding, something h did not think would happen whilst in this dreamscape. He had little time to think, as Levent was already in his personal space and pushed Arnold back with considerable force. Arnold was only just able to stop himself from tumbling over.

"Your pathetic, if this is the best you can do, then you offer little help to me." Levent sneered, his own anger and frustrations now getting the better of him. "You have no chance! In the flower war or against her!"

Levent's insults continued with as much ferociousness as his physical blows, each one chipping away at Arnold. To Levent, he showed nothing, his fists still tightly clenched. He had beaten Levent once and he could do it again. Inside however, Levent's words were slowly chipping away at him, fracturing his spirit and fight ever so slightly with every insult that was thrown at him.

Levent was pacing frantically in front of Arnold, his anger far surpassing Arnold's own at this point. "Do you know the lives that will be lost because of her wrath? That will be on you, because of your inability and unwillingness to learn!" His eyes grew wide as he stopped pacing and turned to face Arnold.

"It's not!" Arnold stood firm, despite buckling inside. "I'm trying"

Levent began clapping slowly, sarcastically, "Well, at least those you care deepest about will have that to keep them safe when their lives are in danger. At least he's trying," Levent spoke sarcastically.

Arnold became lost in his own thoughts. His Mum, Dad and of all his friends were in danger with his Grandma being back and he felt useless. The fate of the Chichen lay on his shoulders and the burden was simply too much to carry.

"Do you even care?" Levent snapped, placing his arms behind his back as he addressed Arnold.

"Of course I do."

"Well 'try' harder! You will lose them all if you don't get a grip on this link to the spirit world. You do not know what that feels like, to be dragged back to this place against your will. To be trapped here for years, to be stolen away from your family and friends; those you love most." Levent's eyes became vacant once more.

Something resonated with Arnold, he could tell that Levent wasn't lost in his thoughts but lost in a memory. For a moment he could see the pain in Levent's face as deep as the scars that he wore. Arnold's own worries about the safety of his friends came charging back to the forefront of his mind, and he could feel his heart beating faster and harder.

"Will she go after my family and friends?" Arnold pressed, his concern growing.

"Look at me!" Levent roared, "Look at my face. She did this to me when I was a child and I was her son. None of them are safe as long as she walks your world freely."

Arnold couldn't help but stare into the deep cracked scars that drew across Levent's face. He had always assumed this was from one of his lions, who he controlled with the blade of the spirits. He had never imagined that it was his own Grandma who had done this to him when he was a child.

"She has instigated all of this in the short time she has been back in this world. She will know everything she wants to about your friends; where they live, their hobbies, everything. She wants revenge against the Chichen and through the flower war, you now stand in her way. You are her enemy and you need to make sure that you see her as one too. There is no redemption for her or for me."

Arnold continued to worry about his friends and his parents. He needed to keep them safe to protect them. His chest continued to pound as if his heart was trying to break free from his body. The sound of a drum beating loudly in his head as his blood pressure continued to rise. Sweat beaded on his head, his mouth becoming dry, and Arnold found himself unable to breathe. He gasped uncontrollably, his body shaking with no control. Try as he may, he continued to struggle to take in air, each second feeling like a minute. His mind over-encumbered with thoughts of the dangers that lay ahead.

What if the Chichen learn about Otto? what if his Dad has another heart attack? Who will look after his Mum if something happens? What about Everett? Can they get back together? What will happen to Marrok and George if his Grandma gets her hands on them? How is he going to survive the flower war?

Arnold fell to his knees and planted his hands against the dry grass beneath him. The air was thicker here, but now it felt as though he was breathing in tar. His head growing fuzzy, he fell faint as he continued to pant for breath, feeling out of control. Staring down at his trembling hands, it took everything he had to stop himself from collapsing into the ground.

"Control your breathing!" As loud as Levent roared, his words sounded muffled to Arnold. "Focus Arnold!"

As Arnold stared down at the ground, his worries continuing to fly around his head, he could have sworn he saw his hands flicker. Closing his eyes for a moment, he stared down once more and saw them flicker again.

"That's it! You're doing it!" Levent's muffled words sounding slightly clearer this time.

Arnold tried to focus, but the world around him was becoming darker, he was still struggling to take in air. He felt a dull thud as Levent knocked him onto his back and crouched beside him.

Levent helped Arnold to sit up as he kneeled next to him to prop him up. "Your breathing is fine. You can breathe fine. You just need to focus" Levent continued to sound muffled to Arnold, but he could understand what was being said to him. "Concentrate on your breathing, in through the nose, out from the mouth." Levent showed what he meant by breathing in slowly through his nose and exhaling through his mouth. "There's nothing physically stopping your breathing. It's all in your head."

Arnold grabbed hold of Levent's arm as panic continued to control his thoughts.

"Listen Arnold, in through the nose and out through the mouth." Levent repeated, demonstrating what he meant once more.

Squeezing Levent's arm, Arnold took a large breath in through his nose before breathing out through his mouth. His breath trembled as he exhaled, but Arnold felt more in control and he continued to repeat the process. The pounding in his chest dulled, the drumming sound in his head subsiding. Arnold's breathing slowly returned to normal until he could breathe freely without having to concentrate on it. All that remained was a splitting headache, which made it difficult for Arnold to keep his eyes open. Arnold felt a flush of heat come over him and he rolled onto his side before vomiting.

"You did it!"

Arnold rolled onto his back and groaned loudly. He felt exhausted. The need for sleep suddenly becoming his biggest priority. He notices Levent was smiling at him, which creeped him out further. He couldn't help but think he preferred Levent in an angered state.

"It's horrible at first but you will get used to it," Levent reassured, he offered Arnold his hand.

Arnold reached up and grabbed it, and Levent helped him back to his feet. Arnold still felt dizzy, and it took a moment for the world around him to stop shaking before he exhaled loudly. "That was horrendous."

"Have a break, then we will go again." Levent grinned.

The thought of going through that again filled Arnold with dread. "Again?" He clarified.

"How else are you going to master this? Whatever you were thinking of then, that is the key to unlocking your link to the spirit world."

Arnold's thoughts went back to his intense training with his Dad when he was learning how to spirit wield. The number of times he had to fail before he could learn to control it, the pain that coursed through his body every time he failed. He wished he experienced that over what he was going through now, but he knew that he was going to have to dig deeper than ever before if he was to have any chance at all in the flower war. Arnold dragged his hands down his clothes to dust himself off before catching Levent's gaze as he readied himself to try again. "Let's go."

Chapter 16

The shrill sound of Arnold's alarm clock startled him from his sleep, severing his connection to the dreamscape. He sat upright before stretching, his back and neck clicking loudly as he did this, and contemplated going back to sleep to rest. The last week had been grueling. His body ached from his training at the Chichen with Mr Whitaker, Kobe and Rosamund. It had been brutal with them, persistently putting him through his paces for combat training. Running through various training, one versus one, one versus two, one versus three. They put him through different training, placing him at a disadvantage, blindfolding him, tying his hands behind his back, tying him up to start off with. These were just a few of the things he had endured during the day which had pushed Arnold harder than ever. Then, as planned, at night time he had been training with Levent to control his ability to spirit walk. He had enjoyed this even less than the physical training, but for each time he tried and triggered his ability, he learnt to control it that little more.

Sliding out of bed, Arnold removed the top he was wearing to get ready for a shower. He examined his torso to see a large variety of bruising decorating his skin. There was one day to go until he would have to travel to an unknown location where the flower war would start and he would meet who he was competing against.

Today he was spending time with his friends and letting his body rest, as advised by Mr Whitaker. It had literally been the longest two weeks of Arnold's life, the time in the dreamscape lasting multiple days whilst he slept. He had used this to his full advantage and felt so much better than he did two weeks ago. His skills had improved drastically because of this intense training and now that he had a day off he didn't fully know how to relax.

After showering and changing. Arnold had spent the first hour of the morning sitting with his Mum and Dad, eating breakfast and talking about normal things. They had agreed the night before that they wouldn't discuss the flower war, knowing the stress this would cause him. For the first time in some time, it felt like a normal morning and for the first time in as long as he could remember Arnold hadn't thought about training, fighting or spirit walking. It had been bliss. His Dad was still on the road to recovery, but everything felt as normal as could be and for a moment Arnold wished that life could stay in this moment.

One thing that Arnold was looking forward to was spending the day with his friends. He hadn't seen them for the last week as he focused on his training and wanted to have a good catch up. They had all agreed to meet at the lockup at ten o'clock and Arnold, for the first time, didn't feel apprehensive about seeing Everett.

Arnold entered the derelict Bramley lockup just before the agreed time. The walk down had been nice, with only a slight breeze in the air. Life had been moving at such a fast pace, it had been nice to slow things down and take everything in. Arnold had been completing mindfulness activities his Mum had told him about, which so far seemed to help keeping him in a calm state. Arnold would normally run to the lock-up for exercise to get there quicker, but he had slowed the pace down and really took in all of his surroundings. He focused on the surrounding noises; he had heard cars, people talking and the laughter of children playing in a nearby park echoing down the street. The gentle breeze pressed lightly against his skin, the air easy to breathe in, compared to when he was in the spirit world. For the first time in a long time, Arnold felt at peace. He felt calm and in a good head space.

Arriving at the lockup, he placed his hand on the side of the container until he felt the familiar pulsating feeling within his palm, followed by the sound of the entrance unlocking. Sliding the door to the side, Arnold stared into the cluttered space. So many of his Grandad's items were here, so many memories. Tears welled in his eyes as his thoughts cast back over everything they had done together and Arnold felt a pang of guilt for what he would think about him training with the man that killed him. The lockup looked neglected and needed tidying. Dust had settled on the piles of books and ornaments. George and Marrok had spent hours putting the books order and his Grandad's journals in date order.

Arnold and the others had spent such a long time in here. It saddened him they had not used it for the last few weeks while he trained and the others worked with the Almec to help Everett get used to wielding Otto's blade.

Moving towards the cabinet in the corner Arnold cast his eyes across the journals that his Grandad had written over his years. He had read all but one, his last journal and it was Arnold's plan to read this before he left for the flower war. He grasped hold of the blue bound journal and tried to blow the dust off the cover, however because of the material he needed to follow this up with a brush from his hand. The dust tickled his nose, forcing out a violent sneeze that almost caused him to knock into one of the vases which stood beside him. *Bloody dust allergy* Arnold thought as he opened the journal and flick through the pages.

Just like the other's the pages contained sketches of spirit beasts, some that Arnold had never heard of before. He could see sections and sections about the Almec. Arnold realised that they often wore the fur or bones of the spirit beast that they were bound too, which wasn't too dissimilar to the eagle warrior armour he had received when he received his rank with the Chichen. The armour wasn't allowed to leave the Chichen and had collected dust for hundreds of years before they gave it to Arnold. The Chichen would rather lock it away so it didn't fall into menial's hands, than share it for people to see and understand. Glancing around the lockup, Arnold scoffed at his own hypocrisy, as the items in his lockup were now doing the same.

"Ey up, he's already here,"

Arnold turned to see Otto and Everett arriving together, which didn't surprise Arnold. The two of them were becoming inseparable since Everett had been given Otto's blade. Otto had been training just as hard as Arnold by the looks of it.

Arnold offered a smile, not wanting either to feel uncomfortable. Otto beamed at Arnold and Everett returned a small smile before looking at the ground and brushing her wiry hair behind her ear, her confidence no longer the same as it once was.

Otto rushed towards Arnold and wrapped his arms around him, squeezing him tightly. "How are you mate?" He asked.

Arnold returned the hug. It was great to see him. They had both been focusing on training so much. Because of Arnold's night-time training in the spirit world; it felt like much longer than two weeks since he last saw Otto and the others. "I'm ok buddy, although my ribs might break if you hug me any tighter." The power in Otto's arms surprised Arnold. "You might just be on a level with Kobe there Otto!"

Otto loosened his hug before stepping away from Arnold "Sorry, don't know my own strength at times."

"What have you guys been up to?"

"Me and Ev have been training with the Almec, Marrok and George too. Kaliska has been showing Ev how to channel my auro through the dagger, she's great with it." Otto beamed as he made himself comfortable and sat on one of the few chairs that they had here.

"I wouldn't say I'm great, but I am getting more comfortable with it. Kaliska has been such a brilliant teacher," Everett corrected him, smiling as she did.

Arnold couldn't remember the last time he had seen her smile properly, not since she lost her spirit beast anyway, and it was refreshing to see. It felt strange hearing both of them refer to Marrok's Mum by name; she was the leader of the Almec and a shaman in her own rights.

Arnold realised this before Marrok had told him through reading the journals that sat behind him. His Grandad had come to be good friends with her, something which the Chichen would have forbidden had they known and potentially exiled him.

"Where are George and Marrok?" Arnold quizzed, thinking the four of them would have come down together.

"Inseparable those two, always together." Otto chuckled, blissfully unaware that this was also the same for him and Everett.

As if on cue, George and Marrok appeared at the entrance of the lockup. The two of them were holding hands as they arrived, nervously smiling at the rest of the group.

"I knew it!" Otto exclaimed, "I bloody knew it! You two are an item." Otto was beaming..

Everett cut a bemused figure and stared at the new couple for a moment. "I thought you-"

"Liked girls?" George cut her off, "I do, well I guess," she stammered "I guess it's more about the personality." She looked up at Marrok and cast him a cute smile. Her cheeks blushed when Marrok returned one back.

"We're happy, that's what's important." Marrok explained, "Neither of us were looking for this, it just kind of happened."

Everett walked towards George and wrapped her arms around her, squeezing her tightly. The two of them hugged, and when Everett spun back around she had tears in her eyes. Arnold wasn't daft and knew that although she was happy for Marrok and George, she would be upset that George hadn't told her beforehand. After all, the two of them had been best friends for years and shared everything.

"Spose we best get each other up to date about the flower war?" Otto blurted out. He had the subtlety of a sledgehammer, and this was one of those moments.

Everett rolled her eyes at Otto before shaking her head, "We were going to at least have a normal morning before we started talking about that. It's what we all agreed."

"It's fine Everett, it's not only me that must compete. Who is it that is representing the Almec?"

"My Mum." Marrok answered, looking frustrated as he explained. "I put myself forward. It would have been an honour, but my Mum wouldn't have it."

"Kaliska? But she is the leader of the Almec?" Arnold questioned. "With the Chichen the Elders can't take part."

"They can. They just have their own rules about who can enter. Any of the clan's involved can participate." George highlighted.

"It's more about protecting those in power." Otto jumped in. "That's why they send a doyen in to do the dirty work for them, then they get the glory." Otto's jaw clenched as he spoke about the Chichen, clearly not approving of their methods.

Arnold looked around the room and for the first time, he felt distant from all of his friends. The four of them were clearly with the Almec and Arnold was the only one there who was part of the Chichen.

"I get it Otto. I understand what they did to you, what the Chichen would do if they were to find out what you can do. Please remember we are not all bad. I want things to be better. Maybe with this flower war we can change things." Arnold tried to explain. The gulf between himself and the others felt huge.

"They won't change, they need to be forced to change." Otto responded, his frustrations not aimed at Arnold, but it was clear they had differing views.

George walked over to Arnold and hugged him. She turned her head towards Otto before speaking, "Just because we are on different sides does not mean that we are not friends first."

Everett joined George and hugged her and Arnold together, "We have been through too much together to let anything impede that."

"Well, isn't this sweet?" The gentle voice of a woman caught the attention of the group, who all turned at once to see who it was.

Standing outside of the lockup stood a young woman. She

was wearing a long, emerald, green coat with the hood raised.

"Erm, can we help you lady?" Otto asked.

Arnold knew who it was in an instant. This was a moment he had longed for when he was a child, but not so much now. Not now he knew what she was capable of. His legs almost went from underneath him and he could feel his heart rate rising.

Not now he thought to himself, recognising the signs of impending panic. He concentrated hard on his breathing, just about managing to keep control of his feelings.

The woman lowered her hood to reveal her soft pale skin, complimented by her long jet black hair. Arnold recognised her dark brown eyes straight away as they were the same eyes that his Dad had and ones that Arnold also shared.

"Are you not going to say hello to your Grandma?" She chuckled. Although softly spoken there was no denying her menacing nature. It seemed strange to Arnold hearing someone who appeared so young referring to themselves as Grandma.

"You!" Acting on instinct, Otto moved in between Arnold and his Grandma. "You need to leave, now!" For a moment, there was what sounded like a growl in Otto's words.

The others had lined up next to Arnold as if the four of them were forming a shield around him.

"Like he said, you need to leave lady." Everett stared intently at her.

"My name's Helen," she smiled. "I am certainly not a lady." Her eyes flickered as she spoke, Arnold could have sworn they appeared more reptilian than human for a moment.

"What do you want?" Arnold bellowed, his voice magnified by the shipping container they were enclosed in.

"Why to make you an offer. When the Calmecac wins the flower war," she paused for a moment, "and they will win. I

125

want you to take your rightful place by my side."

"That will not happen." Otto stepped sideways to block her from looking at Arnold. An act which appeared to irritate her.

"You must be the fabled Night-Sun. Is there not a bone for you to fetch," She said, dismissing him rudely.

Otto's frustrations continued to rise and he clenched his fists tightly, revealing the whites of his knuckles. Everett placed her hand on his shoulder, and Otto seemed to calm in an instant.

"How? Why are you with the Calmecac?" Arnold asked.

"Because the bloodline runs through me, through us should I say." She smiled again.

Everett looked over her shoulder at Arnold. "Don't listen to her. She is toxic, think of everything she has done. She triggered this flower war!"

"Your the one," Helen's smile became even more menacing. "I suppose I should say thank you to you. I can sense it, it was you."

Everett seemed confused. "What do you mean?"

"It was your spirit beast that helped free me from the spirit world. Does that not make you a menial?" She teased.

Everett shook with anger, raising her hand to her hip, where she gripped the hilt of Otto's dagger. She began breathing heavily, her anger getting the better of her.

"Ev don't do it, she's goading you. Listen to me, we don't want to do this." Otto attempted to get through to Everett, but her focus was fixed on Helen. "Ev please, I don't want to." Otto pleaded with her to listen. "You calmed me and I need you to let me do the same."

Everett ignored Otto's plea. "I lost her, I lost who I was. It was all because of you! All of this, everything is because of you."

Helen's eyes widened with joy the angrier that Everett became,

126

her eyes lowered to the dagger on Everett's waist.

"She's not here for me, she's here for Otto! Everett, you need to listen to us." Arnold pleaded, figuring out what his Grandma's plan was.

Everett remained fixed on the woman who she held responsible for losing her spirit beast. "Get her."

Otto's face appeared pained at this command before a glaze overcame his eyes, the same glaze he had when his Dad had been controlling him. He rushed forward towards Helen, his green auro engulfing him like flames. His skin changed appearance and his bones cracked into place as he transitioned into his were-jaguar form. Otto growled loudly as he lunged at Helen, launching a clawed hand towards her. Helen was un-phased by this and grabbed hold of his hand with both of hers, stopping him in his tracks.

Arnold gasped at the sight. She must be much stronger than Arnold had imagined in order to pull off a move like that. Marrok and George ran towards her to assist Otto, Marrok summoning his white wolf and George her fox. Helen used the momentum of Otto to spin before hurling him back toward Marrok and George, he crashed into them like a bowling ball would skittles.

The fight had started so quickly that Arnold hadn't had time to think. He had only briefly seen his Grandma in the spirit world and had spent more time trying to escape the vicious jaws of her dragon spirit beast. Arnold skipped past the others, who lay strewn on the floor. He was sure of her plan, and they needed to stop her. He had to capture her.

Arnold aimed a low kick, which Helen raised her leg to avoid before he threw a punch towards her, which she slapped away with ease. Each strike Arnold made, Helen parried away before grabbing both his arms and kneeing him in the stomach. Arnold's lungs shook as he gasped for air, winded by the blow.

"You're not putting your all into this, I'm disappointed." Helen whispered into Arnold's ear before launching him backwards towards the storage container.

Otto was back on his feet and let out a tremendous roar as he ran on all fours towards Helen. Helen attempted to move out of the way, but Otto's speed caught her off guard and he crashed into her with a flurry of blows. The two of them rolled around the floor for a moment before Helen kicked Otto away and sprang back to her feet like a gymnast. Marrok was behind her and wrapped his arms around her, squeezing as tightly as he could. Sensing an opportunity, Arnold ran towards them and did the same. The two of them were pinning her into position. Both drew on their auro, which engulfed all three of them. The blue and orange power mixing as the two of them used as much energy and strength as they could to contain her.

Helen continued to struggle and seemed surprised at the strength the two of them possessed. She was pressing back against them whilst examining the auro that had surrounded them.

Arnold and Marrok continued to squeeze as tightly as they could when Arnold noticed Everett by their side. She had Otto's dagger firmly in her hand. Anger and hatred filled her eyes and without a word, she aimed the dagger at his Grandma.

"Everett no!" Arnold barked. He had no choice but to let go of his Grandma and grab hold of Everett's wrist, stopping the dagger from plunging into his Grandma's side. "What are you doing!"

Everett had tears streaming down her face as she tried to force her arm forwards but Arnold was too strong.

"Get off me!" Everett cried.

Suddenly Arnold found himself slammed against the ground, the familiar growl of Otto behind him pinning him down.

"Everett, what are you doing?" Arnold pressed.

"I didn't mean for that?!"

Marrok was left struggling left on his own now and Helen began to get the upper hand. George stepped in to take Arnold's place and tried to plug the gap as best she could, wrapping her arms over the top of Marrok, her yellow auro complimenting Marrok's.

Arnold tried his hardest to get up from the floor, but Otto had him pinned face first on the ground. He struggled against him, but Otto was in a better position and was even stronger than the last time Arnold had to go up against him. A searing sting ripped into his shoulder as Otto's claws pierced his skin.

"Everett, you need to stop!" Arnold cried out, "Capture not kill!"

"That's your way, that's the Chichen way!" Everett fired back. "I'm part of the Almec now."

"Hurry Everett! We won't get this chance again!" Marrok encouraged Everett to carry out her task.

Everett made her move and approached Helen to finish what she intended.

Helen smiled at Everett, and her eyes glowed red as her own auro manifested. "Did you really think it would be this easy?" She teased. As her auro grew, so did her strength and she flicked her arms out, forcing George and Marrok's grip to loosen. She rammed both her fists into George's chest, who fired backwards with tremendous force. The only thing stopping her was the derelict storage container that she crashed into.

Everett lunged for her with the dagger, but Helen pushed her back before grabbing hold of Marrok's arms. Marrok tried to pull away, but she was too strong. Helen began looking over at him as if examining him.

"Interesting," she stated. "I recognise that auro, but last I knew it was tethered to a blade." She stared intently into Marrok's eyes before smiling. "I recognise those eyes though. Tell me boy, who is your father?"

"He's dead, he died before I was born." Marrok answered while struggling to break free.

"I think you should speak with your Mum about that. I think someone has been lying to you. Trust me, Grandma knows best." She purred.

Everett threw herself at Helen once more and rushed to use Otto's dagger against her. Helen's face became distorted with rage, her soft demeanor evaporating in a moment and replaced with callous ferociousness. She stepped out of the way whilst dragging Marrok into the path of the blade.

Everett plunged the dagger into Marrok's side, her face recoiling in horror in an instance.

Helen had hold of Marrok from behind, his eyes were wide with the shock at what had just happened. She leaned into his ear to whisper to him, "Speak to your mother, that is if you survive." Before letting go of him. She grabbed hold of the vacant blade that was embedded in Marrok's side and removed it slowly. Marrok grimaced before collapsing on the ground.

Helen looked at the blade and smiled wildly. "That was far too easy." She pointed the blade towards Otto. "Come along, puppy, we have work to do." She turned to leave, calmly and assured as if she had barely broken a sweat.

Arnold felt the pressure on his back ease as Otto was commanded to leave with his Grandma. Arnold sprang up and rushed to Marrok, rolling him onto his back, his hand planted over the wound on his side.

"Everett, what have you done?" He scolded as he removed his t-shirt and pressed it against the wound to slow the bleeding.

"I didn't mean to." Everett was still in shock, her hand covered in blood. "She, pulled him in the way."

"What's going on? Marrok? MARROK!" George had come to and rushed over to assist Arnold. "Everett, pass me my satchel." As she said this, she placed hands over the top of Arnold's, who continued to try and stop the bleeding. Her yellow auro surrounded her hands as she focused her energy to try and heal the wound and soothe the pain for Marrok.

"When did you learn to do that?" Arnold asked.

"Kaliska showed me," she answered. "Everett, pass me my satchel!"

As commanded, Everett reached for George's satchel, which lay at the entrance of Arnold's storage container. She passed this to George, who noticed the blood on Everett's hand. "What did you do?"

She opened the satchel and began to quickly mix some ingredients together to form a paste. "Raise his t-shirt. This will help stop the bleeding, but we need to get him back to the Almec as soon as possible. I think he will be ok, but he needs the healers to help him, they are more powerful than me."

"You hear that? You're going to be ok buddy." Arnold reassured Marrok, who appeared calm.

So much for a quiet last day Arnold thought to himself. Otto was now under the control of his Grandma and Marrok had been wounded badly by Everett. The three of them continued to help Marrok while they waited for the Almec to arrive.

Chapter 17

It had been the strangest of evenings, pretending that nothing had happened when Arnold had got home. But this was the plan that Arnold had decided on and he was now struggling to sleep.

Should he of told his Dad about his Grandma? Should he have told his Dad about Otto? He had a hundred questions in his head and although he had been quiet all evening with his parents, they had assumed this was because of Arnold leaving for the flower war in the morning and not what had happened earlier in the day.

George had insisted that Marrok was going to be ok and Arnold trusted her word. After all, she was quickly becoming a skilled shaman in her own right. Staring into his darkroom, Arnold found himself greeted by nothing but silence and he could not stop tossing and turning in bed. He checked the clock next to his bed; it was a quarter past one and in six hours he would need to get up, get ready and leave to go to an unknown location. He needed to sleep, to rest, but he just couldn't switch off. *What would she want with Otto?* his thoughts continued to buzz around in his head.

Arnold reached for the lamp and switched it on, his frustration not helped with his failed attempts to rest. His phone buzzed quietly next to him and Arnold's heart skipped. He swiped it from the side as quickly as he could to read his message.

It read 'Hey Marrok is doing ok, the healers have done a great job, but he is going to be left with a nasty scar. Kaliska and the others are really not happy about Otto being taken by your Grandma though. G xx,'

Arnold could breathe a sigh of relief for Marrok. He was going to be ok. This helped with some of his worries, but not all of them. *What about Otto? What does she want with him?*

The only thing Arnold was sure of was that whatever she had planned, it wouldn't be good news for Otto or the Chichen. He knew the Almec would be out looking for him, doing everything that they could to return him home. His Grandma knew what she was doing. If her intention was always to get Otto, there must have been a reason for it.

"Levent! Levent!" Arnold's words echoed around the baron field he stood in. He had gotten used to the thick air here now, the first few minutes were always the worst. The nausea would still try to force its way through as Arnold acclimatised to his surroundings. He had all but given up on falling asleep, but finding himself stood in the spirit world meant that it must have happened. Arnold understood that this was his last chance to train before the flower war started and he wanted to use whatever time he had left wisely.

Levent didn't respond to Arnold's frustration, so he took a moment to survey his surroundings. There was a large oak tree on the far side of the field, its bark cracked and scarred. The leaves on the tree were intriguing, a combination of green and orange leaves decorated the branches. The tree was haunting and gave the appearance that it was both dead and alive, piquing

Arnold's curiosity.

Moving through the field, the high, dry grass stabbed into Arnold's legs as he made his way towards the tree. As he approached, he noticed that the lower section of the bark had been stripped away. As he cast his eyes over it and could see that beneath the bark were lashings as if something had been struck against the tree repeatedly. A small stream fell just beyond the tree and Arnold took a moment to listen to the water as it made its escape down its worn path. It felt calm, the heat of the sun warming his skin. To the side, there was a ramshackle hut, the wood heavily decayed. The roof appeared as though it would cave in should there be a slight gust of wind.

Feeling instantly drawn to it, he walked across to the crumbling shed and peered through the broken window. Unable to see clearly, he carried on around the corner until he reached a door which was barely holding onto the frame. Pushing it open the door creaked, echoing loudly inside. Arnold panicked for a moment in case it was inhabited, but then remembered he was in the spirit world. The room was filled with dust; the air felt thick and stagnant as Arnold surveyed the area. There was a sink, a table and a makeshift stool made from the stump of a tree. There was another door at the far side of the hut, feeling curious Arnold made his way towards it. The floor boards groaned and squeaked loudly as he pressed ahead. The fact he didn't fall through them was a miracle. He pressed the door open, unsure what to expect on the inside.

The room was minimalist, with a makeshift bed and a small desk that had been fashioned from some reclaimed wood. The room was just as dust filled as the rest of the house and clearly had not been inhabited for some time. Something on the desk caught Arnold's attention and he went to it straight away. On the side lay a piece of crumpled up paper. Reaching for it, Arnold uncreased the paper so he could see what was on it. To his surprise, it was a drawing of a woman. The detail was incredible, her dark face and eyes accompanied by some form of animal pelt as a headdress. Her smile was radiating and kind. Some of the drawing had become smudged from being screwed up, but overall it was an incredibly detailed picture. Something about this woman felt familiar and Arnold couldn't quite put his finger on it. He opened a small draw which had been attached to the underside of the desk to reveal scores of other pictures stuffed inside. Buildings, temples, artefacts and then Arnold found one which contained a detailed drawing of the blade of the spirits.

"These are Levent's" he muttered to himself. Arnold felt fascinated by the drawings inside. Exploring them, he found further sketches and drawings of the woman and some even older drawings of spirit beasts which dated back to when Levent must have been younger and less skilled because of the childlike details. At the bottom of the pile was another picture, this one again appearing as if a child drew it. It was a picture of where he stood. Arnold recognised the hut, the large oak tree and the nearby stream. Beside the hut stood a stick boy and woman. It was hard to make out what stood next to the stick woman as it had been aggressively scribbled out, with the paper slightly torn. There were speckles of dried blood on the picture too, which felt strange to Arnold. He looked over the picture for a moment before placing it back inside the drawers.

"Make yourself home why don't you," Levent's deep voice was irate. He clearly was not happy with Arnold rummaging through his belongings.

Startled, Arnold spun around to see Levent filling the door

frame. "I'm sorry," Arnold stuttered. "I didn't mean to."

"I hate this place. You think where I am now is a prison. Try spending your childhood here." Levent mused, his eyes becoming distant as he thought over his past.

"Is this her? Is this Grandma?" Arnold held up the drawing Levent had created as a child for reference.

Levent nodded, unable to keep his eyes on the drawing for more than a couple of seconds. "It is amazing what you will accept when you know no different as a child. All I wanted was to spend time with her, but that dragon had other ideas and when it was around it changed her, it controlled her." Levent brought his hand up to his face and ran his fingers over the deep scars that decorated his face.

"What about this one?" Arnold showed Levent the first drawing he had found of the woman in a headdress., "Who is this?".

Levent's response was the opposite of the one in regard to his Grandma. As much as he couldn't stand the sight of the picture he had created as a child, but his gaze was fixed upon this one, as if his eyes were magnetised. There was a long silence between the two as Levent's mind went back to a time long experienced and forgotten. His eyes began to well and Arnold was surprised that Levent could express any emotion other than anger.

"Kaliska," He whispered.

"Kaliska?" Arnold repeated. It was too much of a coincidence. Arnold turned the drawing over to look at it and realised he recognised the headdress. It was that of a coyote, which was the Kaliska he knew's spirit beast.

Levent cast Arnold a quizzical look, "You speak her name as if you are familiar with her."

"We fought with Grandma yesterday. She was too strong for

136

us, though. When she had hold of Marrok, she made a comment about recognising his eyes." Arnold began explaining. "She said Grandma knows best and told him to speak to his Mum about his Dad. At first I thought she was talking to me, but now it all makes sense. Levent, when did you last see Kaliska?"

"Nearly eighteen years ago. I was torn from her and stranded here. They wounded her on our wedding day. The Chichen," Levent's expression was mixed with hurt and anger.

It was too much of a co-incidence, but it was crystal clear to Arnold, the reason his Grandma had made the remark. "Levent, Kaliska is alive. She is the leader of the Almec."

"That can't be," the colour drained from Levent, "I saw her. She died that day. The Chichen, they came for that chalice. They slaughtered everyone." Levent stumbled back at the shock and grabbed hold of the door frame to prevent himself from falling. "How do you know?"

"Because I have been working with her, I am friends with her son Marrok." Arnold explained. "Levent, are you his Dad?"

Levent's eyes darted around the room. He couldn't catch his breath and he made to escape from the room. "No, no, no!" He shouted as he trashed the dining table, flipping it over in one movement. He picked up the tree stump stool and hurled it at the window, which splintered into pieces as it crashed through. "All this time! All this time she has been alive when I thought she was dead!" Levent roared as he kicked out at the front door. The door exploded as it detached from its hinges. He dropped to his knees, staring into his hands, "Everything I have done." He choked up on his words. "I have a son." He brought his hands up to his face and sobbed uncontrollably into them.

Arnold did not know what to do, he had never seen Levent in such a state. His entire world had just been tipped upside down and Arnold couldn't help but wonder what path Levent would have taken had he known about Kaliska and Marrok.

"All this time, all this time I didn't know. She was alive. She survived the attack by the Chichen."

"You said the Chichen slaughtered everyone. I don't understand." Arnold pressed for answers, confused by Levent's statement.

Levent brought himself back to a standing position and turned to face Arnold, "This is what they do, this is what you are part of." Levent spoke slowly, the faint happiness in his voice replaced by the gravel like tone Arnold was more accustomed to.

"That's not the Chichen way, that's not what they do." Arnold couldn't believe what Levent was saying and still didn't fully trust him. However, given the circumstances, he did not believe that he had a reason to lie.

"That is what they want you to believe," Levent looked angry, his face contorting as he explained. "Ironic that they profess to capture, not kill for their enemies, yet they will wipe out entire villages of innocent people as long as they are gaining their precious artefacts. They really would do anything to stop us menials having the faintest of power."

"No, that's not what they do." Arnold spat, refusing to accept what Levent was telling him. "You're lying!"

Levent grinned at Arnold and shook his head, "I am many things boy, but one thing I am not is a liar. Why do you think I am so opposed to the Chichen in everything that I do? They took everything away from me and wiped out the tribe that had taken me in as their own." His eyes became vacant as he lost himself in his memories once more. "I think it is about time that you stopped being so blinkered to the real world. To what

138

your precious Chichen is capable of."

Arnold couldn't help but feel confused. Was this why his Grandad had questioned his allegiance to the Chichen? Was this why he had worked with the Almec? Arnold still did not fully trust Levent or his motives, but his Grandad had his reservations too. Had everything he believed in, in the Chichen, been a lie all this time? Had everything he had been working for all this time been for nothing?

"Listen to me boy, they came for the chalice."

"The one that you used to open the portal in the coal mine?" Arnold questioned.

"Yes, that one." Levent answered sharply. "They came and took the chalice on the day I was to marry Kaliska. The Chichen murdered the shaman, Kaliska's father, and they slaughtered the rest of my tribe like animals. I fought as best as I could, but when I saw them fire an arrow into her, I lost my grip and found myself stuck in this place."

"Except Kaliska survived. She was pregnant when you ended up trapped here." Arnold felt a pang of empathy for Levent's turmoil, hitting Arnold like a train. Never in a million years had Arnold thought that he would train with Levent, let alone understand why he made the decisions that he had done. Why he had walked such a dark path. Levent had no reason to make this up, and Arnold felt his frustrations grow with the Chichen for what they had done. If what they were thinking was true, then Marrok was his cousin. Arnold thought of Kaliska he needed to see her to collaborate what Levent was saying. Then Arnold thought back to the knight he captured Levent in the coal mine. Kaliska was there when Otto brought Levent out of the mines. She saw him and said nothing.

"Tell me everything you know about the Almec," Arnold asked.

The two of them made their way towards the battered oak tree which sat by the stream. They sat for hours as Levent began to further expand Arnold's understanding around the spirit world and the Almec.

Chapter 18

Staring out of the blacked-out window, the road flew past in a blur as they traveled down the motorway. Mr Whittaker sat beside him in stony silence, his open hands placed on his legs as he gathered his thoughts. He opened up his pinstriped suit before placing his hand in the inside pocket and removing a silver pocket watch.

"We should be there soon." He sighed impatiently before rubbing his thumb over the ancient time piece and returning it back to his pocket. "I can't believe this is actually happening. Ethon, you have trained really well these last few weeks. I can't think what is going through your mind now. This contest is going to push you further than ever before."

Arnold wasn't listening, he was focusing on his own thoughts. Although he appreciated the pep talk that Mr Whittaker was giving him. His words sounded like a dull thud in the background, blended with the sound of the car. With his time spent in the dreamscape, it had felt more like six months to Arnold than three weeks; it was time that he was grateful to have had to better hone his skills. Arnold could only hope that the time, effort and pain put in would pay off and prevent him from losing his life. His Mum and Dad had struggled to say goodbye as he left. His Mum had been inconsolable and his Dad gaunt with worry for him. Arnold had been trying in vain to not focus on them, but neither of them could put on a brave face given the concern they had. For all Arnold knew, that may have been the last time he would see them.

Arnold shook his head and snapped himself out of that thought. He could never focus if he started thinking like that and he dragged himself to a more positive mindset. This was by far one of the most difficult things he had ever had to do, and he wasn't even at the destination for the flower war.

"Do you know where it is we are going, Sir?" Arnold's words stuttered out of his mouth, his lips sticking together as he attempted to talk.

"No, only the driver knows the destination which he will have been told just before we set off." Mr Whittaker explained, for a man who liked being in control, he did not appear to be enjoying not knowing where they were going.

It wasn't too long before the car was following the country roads and Arnold couldn't help but feel they were heading somewhere more remote. The view of the motorway was replaced with the green of the trees that lined the roads. They approached a bridge which ran between two large reservoirs which sat motionless on either side of the car. They could see the odd duck paddling around in the cold water.

"Rivington," Mr Whittaker exhaled.

Arnold knew at once where they were and found it strange. After the last few years, he no longer believed in coincidences. Arnold knew at once that this was where the tower was. As far as he knew, its significance remained unknown to the Chichen. The raw energy from the spirit world remained stagnant here, it was where Levent first tried to summon an opening for his Grandma. It was where Levent had killed his Grandad. Arnold felt a burst of guilt, it hit him in his chest like a sledgehammer.

What would Grandad think about me training with the man who murdered him? Would he understand that I have no choice? Arnold knew deep down that he was doing what he needed to in order to survive and felt that his Grandad would hopefully have seen this.

"The ornamental gardens," Mr Whitaker explained, seeming to be reassured by recognising the location. "This is a big place Arnold, no doubt it has been chosen because of the tests you are about to face. When we get there, you will be led to a chamber where you will change into your armour."

Arnold's heart sank, Mr Whittaker's words bringing forth the realisation that this was not a game. Arnold needed to dress in his armour because his life was at risk and he did not know what these risks would be. The car took a turn off the road onto a much slimmer lane. Arnold couldn't help but feel exposed and alone. There were no other cars in sight, no other people, just the distant hills and trees. Ahead of him he could see the foot of a large hill shrouded in trees and Arnold assumed it was here they were heading.

The car followed the lane for around five minutes before it slowed. Arnold's heart pumped faster as his nerves took hold.

"Any words of wisdom before we get there, Sir?"

"Win, at all costs. You must win Arnold, losing is not an option."

This wasn't exactly what Arnold had in mind some more positive words of encouragement would have been more reassuring to Arnold.

Win at any cost Arnold kept playing the words over and over in his head as he approached the location of the flower war.

The car pulled up to a stone hall, which Arnold presumed was where the locals held meetings of importance. Arnold had never seen it before. It must have been a barn or something similar which had been converted. The stone work that had gone into it was impressive. Arnold cast his eyes over the building whilst waiting for Mr Whittaker.

A well-dressed woman approached him. She was wearing emerald green robes which were adorned with many emblems. Strands of her greying hair escaped the baggy hood she had drawn over her head.

"Mrs Stone," Mr Whittaker said as he bowed his head towards her in polite courtesy.

"Mr Whittaker," She nodded politely towards him as she responded. "You must be Arnold Ethon." Her words were short and sharp, less courteous and generally how Mr Whittaker used to greet him.

Arnold knew he was in the presence of the Grand Elder of the Chichen, something that he never thought would happen in his wildest dreams. He did not anticipate such a frosty reception from her, given that it was his life on the line.

"Your life may be on the line," she started as if she had read Arnold's thoughts, "But we have much more at stake here, lose and we will have to hand over power. That just can't happen, it's unheard of." Her focus remained on Arnold and her eyes looked over him as if she was analysing him, calculating his chances all most. "I greet you here as Grand Elder of the Chichen and senior representative of the Grand Council. It is my duty to inform you of your fist task in this flower war."

Arnold's heart sank even further. "Wait what? We're just diving straight in?" This had surprised him.

"Yes, this puts us at a disadvantage given that the Almec's champion is also their leader, meaning she has known in

144

advance what to expect when she first got here." Mrs Stone's lips pursed into a thin line, her skin wrinkling at the side of her mouth as her frustrations were laid bare. "As you can see, we are at the sacred ornament gardens." She cast her hand out to point in the direction of the gardens. "It is here where you will find your first task. Hidden within the ornamental gardens is your sacred armour. Find it and it will equip you for the challenges that await you, don't find it and you will be even more vulnerable than you already are." She cast her eyes towards Mr Whittaker, who was just as surprised as Arnold at the speed the first challenge was being set.

"That doesn't sound too bad. Get in, find my armour and get back to here?" Arnold repeated back loudly, checking that he had the situation right. The first challenge, although catching him off guard, did not appear to be overly complex.

"Be wise not to think that this task will be easy, Ethon," Mr Whittaker warned. "There will no doubt be challenges you will have to face within this task. Keep your wits about you. The second you step foot within those gardens, your life is in danger."

"Mr Whittaker is correct. There are obstacles you will face inside those gardens. Find your armour and improve your chances of winning this war." Mrs Stone turned to head back inside the stone building in front of Arnold.

"Good luck," Mr Whittaker spoke as he left Arnold and moved to follow Mrs Stone inside.

Within a moment, Arnold was alone. He made his way to the path at the bottom of the hill; he needed to find his armour; he needed to win this war.

Suddenly Arnold found himself surrounded by nature, the canopy of trees penning him in. It felt peaceful, almost serene, and calm. There was no noises of cars, bikes, or other vehicles. All that could be heard was the general chat from the birds communicating with one another and the gentle rustling of the leaves on the trees.

Closing his eyes, Arnold took a deep breath to focus himself and concentrate on his tasks. He needed to think about nothing else other than finding his armour. Opening his eyes, he followed the path, the stone barn soon becoming a feature of the past as he entered the natural maze of the forest. Although he had been to the tower that was within the ornamental gardens, he had never explored this place and all he had to go off was instinct. Arnold followed the path for some time, slowly navigating, waiting for whatever obstacles had been put in here for him, but so far he had not come across any. From time to time, he would see piles of stone where walls once lay or parts of the foundations of small, ruined houses. Arnold would check these carefully, but he had so far found nothing to help him with his task. He continued ahead until he could see a stone bridge that sat above the path he was walking on. The bridge was covered in thick, green moss, the stone cracked and loose enough for Arnold to wonder how such a bridge had remained upstanding. Making to pass underneath Arnold reached the shadows that were cast underneath, making it difficult to see clearly.

By the time Arnold felt something press against his leg, it was too late. He had triggered a trip wire; Arnold began sprinting forward, not wanting to wait to find out what the trap was. He could hear something release, splintered wood sprayed around him as sharpened wooden steaks crashed into the walls of the bridge. Within a few seconds, he was clear of the bridge, his heart beating hard against his chest. Arnold turned, looking

146

behind him. Splintered wood lay all over the ground. He had survived the first trap but couldn't help but think he had been clumsy and naive in tripping it.

Stepping back, he cursed as his naivety hit him once more as he tripped over another wire. This time, the enormous trunk of a tree swung down from the side towards him, suspended by ropes. Arnold jumped backwards as the trunk swung past him, barely missing him. Arnold felt the air against his skin, only just keeping his balance. He jumped back as the trunk swung past a second time, not wishing to remain as close as the first time it passed. He turned to face his path once more when he heard a similar noise and realised that another trunk was hurtling towards him he rolled forwards out of the way just in time, as it crashed against the stone that was embedded in the hillside next to him. A low rumble emitted, and Arnold could feel the ground beneath him vibrate. Wondering what it was, he looked above to see the trap had triggered piles of logs to release and they were bouncing down the hillside towards him. With no other option, Arnold sprinted forward with everything that he had. Logs began crashing behind him as they hit the path from above before rolling on down the hill on his right-hand side.

He noticed a section of the path ahead. It had either crumbled away or been removed for this trap. The logs continued to bounce off the floor behind him as he made for the gap. As he reached it, he leapt across it with as much force as he could muster from his legs. He had not realised how large the gap in the missing path was. All he knew was that he did not want to be crushed by the falling logs. Time stood still for Arnold as he hurled himself through the air, unsure if he would make to the other side. He noticed that the hole beneath him was filled with sharpened wooden steaks, designed to maim or kill anyone unfortunate enough to fall in.

Arnold wasn't able to make the length of the gap clearly, he slammed into the side of the opening and grabbed hold of the stone. The stone was loose and came away from the rest of the path. Losing his grip, Arnold fell, reaching out desperately for anything to help him. He grabbed hold of a thick root that had been unearthed under the path and prayed that it would be strong enough to support his weight. To his relief it was and Arnold planted his feet against the wall whilst holding onto it and dragged himself away from the wooden steaks below him. It wasn't the easiest of tasks as the ground was sodden, meaning his footing would slip as he made his way up to safety. When he reached the top, he checked the stone wasn't loose with his free hand before pulling himself up and onto solid ground. He rolled onto his back and exhaled loudly whilst panting heavily to regain his breath.

Arnold didn't wait for long before getting back to his feet. He searched the ground as he walked the path, not wishing to trigger any further trip wires, having only just survived the first set of traps that he had faced. Arnold brushed his hands over himself, clearing off all the debris that had clung to him before carrying on his search for his armour.

Arnold was unsure how much time had passed; it had been a while since tripping the first set of traps and he was still just on edge. Aside from the instant death that Arnold had faced, you would have been forgiven for believing the ornamental gardens were a truly tranquil place. Ornate statues were scattered sporadically. Some barely visible, such was the thickness of the bushes and vines that now wrapped around them, leaving only small sections of the statues uncovered. The baron grounds of the ornamental garden were haunting, the quietness only being disturbed by the gentle rustling of leaves from the trees above him.

The quietness made Arnold feel uncomfortable, the hairs on his arms standing on end at one point.

Arnold continued to navigate the winding paths within the overgrown maze. If not for the current circumstances, his surroundings would be fascinating to explore. Arnold had not expected the danger he faced to be so sudden, but here he was, covered in dirt and grazes and the flower war had barely started. Glancing over his shoulder, the winding path disappeared into the trees. He stopped for a moment, thinking he could hear something scurry past in the bushes to his right. The feeling that something was watching him closely made him feel uncomfortable. He set off down the path once more, surveying his surroundings as he looked for areas where his eagle armour may be hidden.

Ahead of him lay a bridge made of crumbling stone. This one connected the path he was walking on to the far side of the gardens. One side of the bridge had collapsed and fallen down the hillside below. It appeared as though the damage had been caused by something crashing into it, the impact of which must have been tremendous to cause the amount of damage. Reaching the bridge, Arnold scanned over the stone work once more. He didn't trust it one bit, but there was no other way around. He took a deep breath and slowly exhaled before tentatively placing one foot onto the stone; it felt solid, which reassured Arnold slightly.

He left the path and crossed the bridge. His nerves were unsettled. Something did not feel right. Arnold was right to feel this way, and no sooner had he crossed the bridge a bright flash emitted behind him. He knew in an instant that a spirit beast had been summoned. For a moment, he didn't know whether to turn or run. As he turned, a disturbing hiss rang around him and before he could think, he found himself bundled to the floor.

The anaconda spirit beast squeezed him with pure power and Arnold felt powerless. The overbearing feeling of claustrophobia engulfed him as the beast wrapped itself around him. He had never felt power like it, his arms pinned against his sides so tightly that he thought his arm was not far away from breaking. Kicking out was all he could do, and he began thrashing around as hard as he could to make a nuisance of himself as he frantically tried to escape. It was to no avail. As much as he tried, the anaconda would simply roll around, dragging Arnold closer to the crumbled break in the bridge. Arnold realised the anaconda was not trying to crush him, it was trying to drop him off the bridge.

Arnold continued to struggle but he was slowly pulled towards the sheer drop below. Closing his eyes, Arnold focused. He couldn't maneuver his hands, but his body began emitting a deep blue glow. A shriek echoed down the hillside as his eagle burst from within him. His eagle did not wait, knowing the danger Arnold was in and flew above him and the Anaconda. Arnold glanced up to see his eagle in the sky. The sun cast behind it perfectly. Had he not been in this situation, he would have enjoyed the sight, but he continued to fight against the powerful beast with every ounce of strength that he could muster. The eagle swooped down and plunged its talons into the side of the anaconda, which made an unnatural shrill noise as it recoiled in pain as the talons pierced its skin.

In an instant, the pressure relieved from around Arnold's arms and he found himself able to breathe freely again. Taking a huge gulp of air, he began coughing, becoming light-headed from the sudden release of asphyxiation.

There was only a moment's reprieve however, with the anaconda quickly adjusting itself and turning to face Arnold once more. It began sliding along the ground far quicker than Arnold would have liked. They were still on the bridge, the crumbling hole beside him still too close for comfort. Arnold shuffled backwards in anticipation, he had no idea what to do next, he had no weapon to protect himself. All he had was his spirit beast

is this the test? he thought to himself. He closed his eyes and tried to focus on his spirit companion.

When he opened them, he was not face to face with the anaconda but looking down on himself. It was a bizarre experience and one that Arnold would have appreciated had he not been in such immediate danger. He wasn't in control but more a passenger, knowing instantly he was looking through the eyes of his spirit beast. The last time this had happened was when he was meditating with Mr Whittaker, when he nearly unlocked his power for the first time. Although not in control, Arnold felt as if he could feel what his spirit beast could feel, the sensation of the air pushing against his feathers, the exhilaration of gliding. His spirit beast tucked its wings in beside it, its velocity picking up as it started hurtling towards the anaconda that continued to move at speed towards Arnold. The anaconda opened its jaws to reveal its gaping mouth as it struck out at Arnold. His spirit beast continued to dive towards his attacker, unrelenting at the speed at which it approached.

Pull up, you're going to hurt yourself

There was no time, his spirit beast smashed into the side of the anaconda, Arnold jolted and his eyes snapped open. A flurry of limbs scrambled around the floor ferociously as the two spirit beasts fought with fury. The two separated, the anaconda opening its mouth wide as a threat, his eagle spreading its wings. Arnold noticed that one wing stooped slightly lower, having injured itself in the initial impact. Its wingspan was still impressive and its position would imply that it was shielding Arnold from the attacking beast. They continued in a standoff. Each time the anaconda lunged forward, the eagle would flap its wings, putting the anaconda off. As the anaconda lunged once more, the eagle flapped its wings enough to leave the ground slightly and landed on the side of its foe. The anaconda wriggled around, but the force Arnold's spirit beast was applying was enough to stop it from moving. His eagle studied it for a moment before lunging its beak down towards the anacondas' eyes. The noise that the creature emitted pierced Arnold's ears. The eagle began flapping its wings and took flight slowly, clasping its talons tightly as the anaconda flailed around powerless. Arnold's beast moved towards the edge of the bridge and, once past the fractured stone wall, it released its talon, leaving the anaconda to its fate as it disappeared over the edge.

Arnold's sides were throbbing. As he breathed in, he winced. The pain didn't feel like a broken rib, but at the very least, they were badly bruised. His eagle landed by him and shuffled closely. Feeling the warmth against him immediately made the pain in his ribs subside. He knew that as long as he had his companion by his side, he would be ok. Arnold felt safe and for now he needed to rest for a while before continuing his search for his armour.

Chapter 19

Arnold felt comfortable, so much so that he could have fallen asleep sat against the far side of the stone bridge. It had been around an hour since his showdown with the anaconda and he had spent this time with his spirit beast next to him, letting his body heal from the fight. His eagle perched beside him. It held an extended wing around Arnold, offering him shelter from the icy breeze that had steadily been picking up. Their blue auro surrounding them both, a soft pulsating feeling coursed around Arnold's body, bringing him further comfort. This process offered not only Arnold pain relief, but it also helped him calm his mind. His thoughts felt, more rationalised, like he could allow himself to think, to breathe. He wished he could stay in this moment for longer, but knew he had already spent too long here. He dusted himself down once more before standing up. Arnold placed his hand onto his eagle, who bowed the crown of its head to allow him to do so. They shared this moment for a few seconds before his spirit beast dissipated back into Arnold. Once gone, all that remained was a dull ache in Arnold's ribs, which paled compared to what he had felt just a short time before.

The overgrown gardens were proving far more dangerous that Arnold had thought they would be. His life could have already been ended twice, and this was before he had even found his armour. He didn't dare think about what they lined up for him once he had his armour. What he did know, given what he had faced so far, he looked forward to being in possession of his armour and being that little bit safer. The search was more laborious than he had thought, with the ornamental gardens proving a far bigger maze than he imagined. Continuing through winding paths, Arnold passed the decrepit foundations of a crumbled stone building. Its former glory no longer on display to the world. All that remained now was a stone grave. Arnold knew as soon as he passed it for the third time that something was a miss. Having headed straight and right at the path further ahead, they had both brought him back to this point. Arnold could feel his frustrations growing.

This is just stupid Arnold thought to himself, turning as he passed the rubble for the third time. Arnold wondered if he was now destined to be here forever, destined to be stuck in this endless loop. On the fourth time of circling around, Arnold couldn't help but curse loudly. He must have been walking for hours and as he pulled up next to the crumbled building again, he let out an enormous sigh.

What am I meant to do? He wondered as he examined the grey stone that formed the base of the house. There was a green tinge to most of the stone, the thick moss that had taken up residence binding what remained of the building together. As he kept coming back to the building, Arnold concluded that perhaps he should examine the building further.

Stepping onto the foundations, Arnold could see the base of the building in its entirety, the stonework on the ground highlighting where the rooms would have once been. In the corner of the foundations, something caught Arnold's eye.

154

There were some loose stones piled up which stood out to him. These stones were clean, there was no dark green moss clinging to them like an unwanted blanket. They had been moved; they had been placed there and Arnold wanted to know why. Moving towards the stone, Arnold grabbed the first piece with both hands. It was rough to touch, the coldness of it touching his bones. He tossed it to the side and continued to remove more heavy stones until it revealed a trap door underneath. Arnold's eyes widened and he breathed a sigh of relief before cursing himself for not figuring this out sooner. How much time must he of wasted walking around in circles? He couldn't help but feel that those observing would have a laugh at his expense, at his in experience.

The trap door comprised of wooden slats, not all of them were fully intact. Bending down, Arnold reached for a gap in the wood and took hold of the edge of the door, pulling it towards him. Some of the wood turned to dust in his hands, but Arnold kept hold of the door and lifted it up to reveal a passageway underneath. Arnold felt a blast of warm air hit him in the face. It was a welcome feeling, given how long he had been outside. That was until the musty air slapped him in the face. Arnold couldn't describe the smell, other than it smelt old. Knowing the path he needed to take, Arnold lowered himself into the passageway, the darkness engulfing him in an instant. The light from above trying to force its way through the gap but failing miserably. The darkness ahead was surprising and daunting. Arnold contemplated using his aura to light his surroundings, but he didn't want to draw on his energy if it could be avoided. He skimmed over his surroundings and could see that an old torch was fastened to the wall. Arnold knelt down, finding pieces of flint on the ground. He couldn't help but feel that this was all too easy, too much of a coincidence that what he needed was here. He brought the flint up to the torch and hit the two pieces together forcefully. After a few attempts, a spark connected with the torch and suddenly his immediate environment was engulfed with light.

Clasping the torch tightly in his hand, Arnold removed it from the stand that fixed it against the wall. The warmth of the flame pressed harshly against his cheek so he held it away further from him as he began his descent into the darkness. Taking each step tentatively, Arnold continued reluctantly, his mind instantly transported to the coal mine which he had explored in Oswald. This was worse, though. The passageway he was walking through was narrow and Arnold could feel the sense of claustrophobia worsening. It wasn't too long before there was a fork in the passage way and he had a decision to make, left or right.

Arnold took the right turn instinctively, not knowing why he made this choice but committing to it none the less. The walls felt like they were becoming narrower, but Arnold could not tell if this was the case or if his mind was playing tricks; he brought his hand up to his face to brush off another wave of cobwebs that he walked into. The sooner he got out of here, the better. Arnold continued at a steady pace, his heart rate increasing the longer he was down here.

Underfoot the ground wasn't even and now and then Arnold would stumble as his feet would clip stones that protruded from the ground. As he stumbled again, he heard a scurry beside him, which was not the sound of the stone and dirt on the ground. He froze, looking for where the sound came from. His heart sank as he saw a gigantic rat. Arnold simply wanted to be back outside, the rat causing more anxiety for him than the giant anaconda he had had to fend off just a short time ago.

As he concentrated on moving forward, something changed in the passageway. Suddenly, the air felt thicker. It was a strange sensation and because of the darkness, Arnold could have been forgiven for thinking he had inadvertently phased into the spirit world.

This felt different somehow, there was a sudden pressure he could feel and his eyes stung. The sting you only really understood when you swam too deep in a swimming pool. This is what he was experiencing. The passageway rumbled as dirt fell from above him. Arnold looked behind him and in the distance he could see an abnormal turquoise glow. Because of his enhanced sight, Arnold could see it was a flame like those that he saw when undertaking his ch 'ahb'. To his horror, the flames were moving in his direction and far quicker than he liked.

Arnold set off at pace down the passageway, his legs burning as he pushed himself as hard as he could. He couldn't see further than a meter in front of him, illuminated only by the torch, he gripped it tightly as he continued to escape the unnatural flames which continued to follow him. He saw stars as he clattered into the wall of the passageway as he reached a sharp left turn he hadn't seen. The torch spiralled out of his hands. Realising he didn't have time to pick it up, Arnold instinctively emitted his auro, which illuminated his immediate surrounding. It wasn't long before the flames crashed into the dirt behind him as he continued to sprint away from the danger; the ground rumbling more violently as the flames drew closer. They did not move like you would expect flames to. Its motion was more in common with that of water cascading down an overflowing river. The ground continued to grumble as if walking on a live volcano, Arnold feeling like the passage could engulf him from below at any moment.

A swarm of rats gathered ahead of him as they also attempted to escape the green energy that was chasing them. Their squeaks growing louder as they became more frantic, their nails scratching against the dirt as they became more desperate to find an exit.

Arnold could feel the heat of the unnatural flames licking his back, the warmth stung against his sodden t-shirt. After another sharp turn, Arnold couldn't help but feel that he was only avoiding the inevitable. These flames were going to catch up with him. Then he spotted a flicker of hope, an opening further down the passageway. He could see a beam of natural light. His heart was racing, his legs were aching and tired, and his back was burning. Digging as deep as he could, he continued his sprint, the wall of death right behind him. If he was to fall now, then the flames would engulf him. Staring at the light, he used this to motivate himself and his gaze was now firmly fixed on his way out of here. Dirt continued to fall from above as the ground beneath him rumbled aggressively. He gave one last burst of energy as the natural light drew closer and closer. As he reached the end of the passageway, the flames were on him. Arnold dived for cover as soon as he knew he was outside, the green flames roaring as they burst out into the open air. A flash of white engulfed his vision as his eyes adjusted to being free of the darkness. He lay on his back, staring at the trees above him as they came into focus. He took a huge gulp of air and allowed himself a moment to appreciate the sound of the birds conversing in the trees, oblivious to what he had just been through.

His back was stinging, and he knew that the flames had caused some level of burning to his back. The burning sensation began to more than sting and Arnold winced as he brought himself back to stand up. Arnold was still panting, as he looked into the void he had just run through to see the last of the flames disappearing back inside. He did not know what had caused the flames, but knew they were linked to the spirit world. The exit itself was carved out of the dirt and a decrepit tree sat atop of the hole with its old roots wrapped around the opening as if it was holding the passageway open. This place was a death trap and Arnold wondered how such a tranquil place had been transformed into such a space where life could be taken so easily. When all this was done, Arnold vowed to himself that he had no intention of ever returning to this place and welcomed the moment where he could leave. The air tasted sweet as Arnold looked around to gather his bearings, unaware of where he now was within the gardens.

The canopy of trees above him was as dense as ever, with only flashes of light entering. The surrounding ground resembled stained glass from the speckles of colour, hitting some of the translucent leaves, leaving an assortment of colours like a kaleidoscope.

Arnold was exhausted now, but he knew he needed to carry on. Tentatively, he continued towards the only opening within the trees that looked as though he could pass through.

It wasn't long before Arnold noticed a slight limp when he was walking. His spike in adrenaline had subsided, meaning that the aches, scrapes and burns felt worse than before. He needed to rest his ankle, which he knew caused the limp he was carrying, but he didn't dare stop. The pain wasn't unbearable but it meant that he wasn't functioning at a hundred percent and Arnold needed to keep his momentum going if he was to find his armour.

Arnold had now lost all semblance of time and did not know how long he had been in the ornamental gardens for, the light was slowly fading as dusk set in. Arnold breathed a sigh of relief as the trees thinned and ahead of him lay an open field. At least out of the trees, he wouldn't feel as on edge. He could defend himself better in the open in the denser woodlands.

As he approached the larger expanse of land, he could see something in the distance on the far side of the field. It was a shelter made of large chunks of stone. *no doubt another ornamental piece* Arnold thought to himself. The front of the shelter was completely open, the opening was lined with metal bars which seemed to be fixed into place, like a prison cell. As the sun lowered, its light caught something that reflected at Arnold. His heart skipped a beat as he realised that he had finally located his armour. With a fresh wave of motivation, Arnold began making his way across the field, the pain in his ankle less noticeable as he hobbled across the land at a quickened pace. With each step he took, he could his heart skipping faster than his spirits lifted. He had found his armour. Despite his age and inexperience, he had already proved any doubters wrong. But then he realised, he may have found his armour but he would still have to gain access to the building. Something sat in the back of Arnold's mind like a heavy weight. Given what he had already faced, it would be too easy to walk up to the stone shelter and collect his armour. He knew there would be a catch, another test that he would have to face.

It wasn't long before he had reached the shelter. To its side sat a small sign which explained what the monument was.

'Dragon's Keep' Arnold read aloud. 'Brilliant, just what I need, another dragon to contend with' Arnold sighed to himself as he patrolled the front of the keep examining the jail like bars that blocked his way in. The light of the day was fading fast, Arnold focused, his auro emitted a soft blue glow around him, which lit up the surrounding grounds. He could see clearly into the keep now and he smiled as his eyes fell upon his armour, on the other side of the bars. It was out of reach, but just seeing it made Arnold feel safer. Other than his ceremony, when he was granted the rank of eagle warrior, he hadn't worn it. Because of its age, Arnold had been told he could not train in it either. The metallic chain mail was decorated with feathers of eagles, the fact that the feathers did not look old or aged led Arnold to believe that they possessed a mystical energy.

It was impressive to look at, the intricate detail of the stitching and joining of the feathers left Arnold in awe. He remembered how light it was to wear, which had surprised him. At the top sat the headpiece for the armour the part that Arnold had found the most uncomfortable, only because it limited his vision. This was because of the beak like shape which protruded over the top of his head when he had worn it. The helmet too had smaller feathers connected to it, it seemed to give off a soft blue glow as Arnold's auro touched it.

To the right of his armour Arnold saw the hilt of his machuahuitl and he wished he could reach through and grab it, he would certainly feel a lot safer with it in his hands. He was so close, and it frustrated him he couldn't get through the bars.

"Enjoying the view?" A voice called from behind Arnold, startling him.

Arnold spun to see who it was, three men, and a woman stood in formation just a couple of meters away from him. He recognised two of them in an instant. It was the thugs that they had come across whilst camping in the lake district.

161

"Gregor isn't it? And Mik, Mik, Mikel?" Arnold addressed the unmistakable hulking frame of Gregor and the rat like features of Mikel. The two could not have been more polar opposite to one another. The third man was stood more imposing than Mikel and he had long black hair which was tied back. His face was a combination of scars, poc marks and grimaces. The woman that stood with them was slender with short red hair. One of her ears was lined with studded piercings and her left arm covered in tattoos. All four of them had some form of armour on, and weapons in their hands.

"Welcome to your last test" The woman whispered, in a well-spoken accent. Arnold knew that despite her feigned politeness, this was going to progress to a highly dangerous situation.

"Test?" Arnold questioned fiercely. "Then why does this feel more like a trap, like everything else I have faced in here?"

The woman smiled gently, holding a dagger in each of her hands made her grin even more menacing. "Believe it or not, this is part of your trial within this flower war," she explained.

"Doesn't look or feel that way," Arnold shrugged.

"Valin was asked to pick four of us to guard your armour." Gregor piped up.

"We have been told we can do whatever we want to stop you from getting to it." Mikel grinned callously.

The air was charged with tension as Arnold's four opponents stared at him with wicked determination. Four against one was going to be a near impossible task, but Arnold knew he had no other option. They all had weapons and some form of armour. Arnold had nothing, his weapon and armour were behind him.

The man that Arnold didn't recognise let out an inpatient roar as he charged towards Arnold, a spiked club held in both hands as he moved towards him. The other three stood back to watch the spectacle. They wanted to play with their prey; they wanted to tease him.

Arnold had expected all four to come at him at once, but he was grateful that they didn't. Arnold waited for the opportune moment, which arrived when the man swung his club at him. The man was quite large, and this affected his speed. Arnold ducked before breaking into a roll to create some space between the two of them. The man swung at him again. Arnold sprung backwards out of the way as the club swung past once more.

"Come on, Prious," the woman cheered. "He's teasing you."

"I can handle the boy Marissa." He replied, his eyes fixed on Arnold. He raised his club above his head and brought it down towards Arnold. With no other option Arnold changed tactic and this time stepped into Prious's space. His knuckles cracked as he tensed his fists tightly, they cracked even louder as he struck Prious under the jaw. Prious tumbled backwards from the blow, clearly dazed. Arnold took a step back before launching himself at his opponent and vaulted into the air, bringing his knee to his face. The crunch was satisfying to Arnold and Prious let out a grunt before falling onto his back,his club flying from his grasp. He was down and out, his nose bloodied and broken.

one down three to go Arnold thought to himself as sweat beaded on his head. It was better odds now, but they still outnumbered him.

"Not bad kid," Mikel jeered. "Prious was the weakest out of us, less skilled should I say." He grinned wildly as Gregor and Marissa stepped forwards towards Arnold, with a dagger in each hand, Gregor with what looked to be a morning star. He let go of the spiked metal ball in his hand, which was attached by a chain to the hilt that he held in the other. Arnold had read about them but never seen one, nor had he ever practiced against this kind of weapon. His chest pounded wildly as his attackers made their next move. This time, both rushed at him.

Marissa reached Arnold first and took a swipe at him with her dagger. Arnold jumped back. Gregor swung the morning star at Arnold, who ducked the blow. His heart beating even faster and harder, he thought it might burst out of his chest.

They were trying to kill him and Arnold was defenceless. He backed away until his back made contact with the metal bars of the dragons keep behind him. With nowhere to go, Gregor swung his morning star at Arnold once more, who ducked it again. It was far too close this time and lucky for Arnold, the chain wrapped around one of the bars. Arnold threw a flurry of blows at Gregor, but his fists seemed to just bounce off his head. Gregor was a man mountain, and he let go of his weapon and gripped Arnold by the throat. Arnold continued to strike him, but he was powerless against him. He could slowly feel his feet leaving the ground as Gregor picked him up and pressed him back against the bars. Arnold's heart rate peaked; his eyes bulged as he threw everything he had into striking Gregor's arms. His head became fuzzy as he could not breathe, his blows becoming weaker as he slowly ran out of energy.

Something lit up inside Arnold and he felt Gregor's grip loosen, the world around him becoming littered with an unnatural haze. His enemies had vanished, but his surroundings remained the same. Although the rusted iron bars of the keep were not present in the spirit world. Arnold stepped inside, before waiting for the feeling he had learned to watch for. It felt like the pull of a magnet in his stomach and he waited until he could feel it, then focused. The air felt normal once more and metal bars stood solidly in between Valin's thugs and Arnold.

"What in the blazes" Gregor cursed.

"How did you do that?" Marissa hissed, her eyes widening at what she had just bore witness to.

Mikel joined them to examine what was going on. "How did you get in there?"

"Unnatural magic," Marissa alleged. "Tell me boy, are you a shaman?"

Arnold panted as he regained his breath. He felt a surge of anger towards the three of them, an anger that he hadn't felt for some time. They were cowards. The rules of the flower war had stipulated that they were to stop Arnold at all costs, but with four of them, did they really need to kill him? His auro was connected with the spirit world now and Arnold needed to use this to his advantage whilst he could. He turned to face his armour which stood on a stand and reached for the hilt of his machuahuitl that sat beside it on a plinth.

His free hand began glowing in an instant as he slapped his open palm against the top of his weapon. Raw energy charged around him, which caused the leaves and dirt on the ground to raise in the air around his feet. Arnold could feel the energy coursing through him and he tensed his muscles tightly, not wanting to lose his grip. The last thing he needed now was to end up in a convulsing heap on the floor. It was difficult to control, but Arnold had practiced and developed the skill of spirit wielding now. He pulled his hand away from the hilt to reveal his auro formed machuahuitl blade. Its glow was haunting and the keep was now fully illuminated, the shocked expressions of his enemies a priceless picture.

"Valin never said you could do that" Marrissa seemed frustrated and intrigued, as if she was studying an animal in the zoo. Her hair was being blown back from the force of Arnold's energy.

Arnold continued to focus his auro as the raw energy from the spirit world coursing through his body. It felt as though gravity was trying to pull him to the ground. Simply standing up took a lot of focus and now he had to see off these foot soldiers of the Calmecac. He closed his eyes once more and waited for the sensation to engulf him; the pull was intense and his body felt as though it was vibrating inside. He opened his eyes, knowing he was in the spirit world. The iron bars of the dragons keep were gone as he walked the spirit plains. He stepped forward, knowing precisely where Marissa stood staring at him. He cleared his mind and thought about his parents; it was what brought him back last time, and he hoped it would work again.

It did, and in a moment he was back and stood beside Marissa.

"How did you?" She stuttered, her mouth agape at what she had just bore witness to.

Arnold didn't waste any time as he shoulder barged her into the bars before bringing the hilt of his machuahuitl and ramming this into the face of Gregor, who also cut a bemused figure. Mikel brought the axe he was wielding down but Arnold was quick and raised his spirit blade around to block this. The weapon was almost weightless, but it was unbreakable, providing Arnold remained focused and concentrated on his energy.

Mikel was strong and pressed down against Arnold's weapon harshly, his teeth bared as he pressed against him with all his might. The other two had shaken off their initial shock and were regrouping to fight back. Arnold focused and in an instant, he was back in the spirit world. He stepped to the side before moving behind where Mikel was before focusing on his parents again. In a flash, he snapped back and was standing behind

Mikel; he launched himself into the back of him, an audible crunch could be heard as Mikel's head snapped back. His axe came bearing down on Gregor, who had to jump to the side. Marissa was less fortunate, and the two of them clattered together. Gregor's size meant that Marissa was sent crashing to the ground. She wailed as she skidded across the dirt. The bars rang and Mikel bounced into them. Gregor adjusted and swung his club at Arnold once more. As quick as a blink, Arnold vanished from in front of Gregor's eyes, his face was a picture of frustration and anger. Arnold appeared beside him again and crashed a tightly clenched fist into the side of his face before disappearing again. In a moment he was on the other side of him, only this time, as Arnold appeared, he was already swinging a blow, which he slammed into the other side of Gregor's face.

Gregor roared in anger, unable to see Arnold for long enough to strike him. Arnold appeared in front of him this time, truly getting used to his spirit walking, and brought his spirit blade down against the club that Gregor clung to like a safety blanket. It splintered in two, Arnold's weapon cutting through it like a warm knife to butter. Gregor gurned at the site, but before he had time to blink, Arnold had vanished once more. Arnold gave a quick jab with his left hand before cracking the hilt of his machuahuitl into Gregor's face. He groaned before falling backwards and slumping to the floor.

Arnold swung his blade to meet Mikel's axe and set off with a flurry of strikes. Mikel was on the back foot.

"Do you yield?" Arnold roared, his heart racing. He could feel the raw energy engulfing his body more aggressively.

Mikel snarled, gripping his axe with both hands. "I'll not yield to a mere boy!" He began swinging his axe wildly.

Arnold brought his blade up to parry his attacks. Mikel's onslaught continued, but Arnold could keep himself safe. Mikel's eyes glanced to behind him and Arnold knew what was coming. He shifted into the spirit world again and out of sight, stepping to the right before returning. Marisa was lunging at the spot where Arnold stood only a second ago but her blade was heading straight towards Mikel, whose eyes had widened in terror.

Arnold bolted forward and knocked the dagger from Marrissa's hand, just before it plunged into Mikel's chest. Marisa swung her free arm at Arnold, but he grabbed hold of her arm before slamming his elbow into her face forcefully. She stumbled before Arnold spun into a kick which connected with her chest. Marisa landed on the ground sprawled out, she lay struggling to get her breath. Arnold could tell from the noise that she wasn't getting up. She had a broken rib. Arnold faced Mikel, his face beaded with sweat, panting and exhausted.

Mikel stared him down and continued to squeeze the shaft of his axe with both hands, readying himself for his next strike. "You saved me," He stuttered. "Her dagger was about to hit me. You saved me even though we have tried to kill you." Mikel stuttered.

Arnold readied himself for the next strike, but as the two of them panted like dogs, the attack didn't come. They continued to stare each other down, but neither made a move.

"I yield," Mikel announced, dropping his weapon on the ground.

His actions surprised Arnold, but it was a welcome reprieve. He waited a moment to assess if Mikel was being honest. Convinced that he was, Arnold let the energy he was channeling through the machuahuitl fade, until it vanished. An icy shiver ran up his arms as if there was ice in his blood, a sensation Arnold had become familiar with when spirit wielding.

He had somehow beaten the four of them, his training with Levent proving useful. There was no way that he would have survived that duel had he not pushed himself with his intense training and he was grateful that he had. All Arnold wished for now that he had gained his armour was to rest. It had been an intense day, and he felt exhausted. Arnold could only dream of being allowed to rest after everything he had been through today.

Chapter 20

It had been a long day; she had been waiting for news of her grandson for hours with nothing to be heard. Word had broken earlier of Kaliska and Valin, who had both been successful in locating and gaining their armour.

Sitting in a small, darkened room, she mused over her thoughts as her plans slowly unfolded. A small fire was lit in the wood stove, bringing a calmness to the room. There was no need for distractions such as a TV when a fire was lit and she stared deep into the flames as they danced around. The charcoaled wood cracked loudly, so she leant forward to pick up a metal bar, she stoked the fire until some fresh flames grew from the ashes. She followed this up with a fresh piece of wood, which she placed on the top of the fire delicately. She continued to stare into the charred pit, her eyes vacant as her mind drifted o distant memories.

They deserve what's coming A voice hissed in her mind as clear as someone was to be in the room with her.

They deserve every semblance of pain for what they have done to us it continued aggressively. Its voice was rasping, as though in a state of constant pain and rage.

She continued to stare deeply into the flickering flames, memories snapping into the forefront of her mind. Thoughts of a walk in the park, holding her child's hand, having a picnic. Then a memory of her screaming pushed through the nice memories, begging for him not to trigger the portal. The one that trapped her for so long.

They left us, they trapped us! The voice boomed. *We need to do this; they need to pay.*

She felt vacant as she continued to stare into the fire; the embers cracking loudly as they burst. For very brief moments, these memories would return to her. In a moment, they would be gone. Replaced with the dark memories of her past, reminders of the wrongs she had faced. She hadn't been given a trial, no chance to explain that she could control her spirit beast. Instead, her husband had banished her to the spirit world along with any hope she had once had of controlling the beast. It was that act of betrayal that had tipped her anger past the point of no return. It was at this point that the dragon truly took over, that she let it in fully and it corrupted her. This is where she had become a mere passenger in her own body. It was all their fault. Had the Chichen not been how they were, if only their own people knew what they were capable of. The cruelty they show to those that cannot control their abilities, the pain they inflict when taking what doesn't belong to them.

It was Hershel's fear of what they would do to her that pushed him into thinking that being trapped in the spirit world was a better option than falling into the hands of his Chichen. Even though he had been driven by fear and did what he thought was best, he was just as culpable. Without his and his friend's actions she wouldn't have fully lost control, she wouldn't of spent an eternity walking the plains of the spirit world.

We are glad he's dead the rasping voice stung her eyes with its sharpness. Their thoughts were shared. Her mind couldn't escape without being followed by her spirit beast. Memories, thoughts, emotions bonded so tightly between the two that she didn't know what was her own and what was the dragons. She didn't know which was the worst prison, being trapped in the spirit world or being trapped in this body.

A single tear escaped her eye. It ran the full length of her emotionless face. It felt warm against her skin until eventually falling and landing on the dark wood floor; staining the dry wood where dust had collected.

Moments like this were a rare thing indeed. Anger was the emotion she showed. It engulfed her all the time. It was anger that had kept her motivated to escape, the chance of vengeance against everyone.

And now here she was, her plan set into motion, and what did she find? Not the satisfaction that she had yearned for, but distant memories and thoughts trying to push their way through. Since the day she stepped through that portal and back into this world, they had been returning in short, sharp bursts.

They will the voice hissed once more *Pay for what they have done to us. They will know fear like we have known anger like we have shared.*

A sudden tap at the door jolted her mind back into the room and her expressionless face contorted into a forced grimace.

"Come in." She summoned them. Given the time, she hoped it was news of how the day's events had played out.

A scrawny, balding man entered the room. He wasn't very tall, and his wrinkles appeared to overlap on his forehead, his eyes barely visible. He was wearing a tatty black robe with gold thread, his sandals poking out from the bottom of the robe. The fear in him was apparent as he entered the room. He didn't want to be there any more than she wanted him to be there. It was more out of necessity than a want; he had information that she needed and he had a duty to keep her updated.

"The boy has returned, albeit battered and bruised. But he has returned with his armour like the others." His voice was shrill, and he spoke slowly, like a creaking floorboard.

"He managed to beat four of them?" Her response was quick and sharp. She had sent more people to defend the armour than the Chichen and Almec had. Still, four adults could not beat the boy, yes he wasn't far off an adult and yes, he was more powerful than anyone else of that age. She was surprised four of Valin's foot soldiers could not stop him. His involvement in the flower war was not something which she had calculated when putting this plan together. He was the one person who could ruin everything.

"He has set tongues wagging in the chambers of these grand halls," the man explained. His body language was like that of a dog wanting its belly rubbed for doing something positive.

"Do tell." She didn't have time for idle gossip, nor getting into a lengthy conversation with this weasel.

"It would appear the boy has a hidden power." His words stretched longer than they naturally should.

The way he spoke irritated her tremendously. "Spit it out". She stared at him intently, needing to know what he was talking about.

"Tongues were wagging at how he could learn how to spirit wield, something that is normally achieved after years of practice and mastery. This evening he has displayed an ability never seen before." His hands held together in front of him, his fingers intertwined uncomfortably.

"Will you just tell me!" Her rage was coming to the forefront and her voice trembled as she barked at the man. What on earth had the boy done now? He was becoming a serious thorn in her side. She had waited too long for her vengeance and it wasn't something she was prepared to miss out on because of him.

The man jumped back, startled by her aggression, his hands clearly shaking as he stuttered his words. "He could use his energy to disappear and reappear quickly. He used this ability to not only gain access to the keep where his armour was stored but to dispatch the warriors you had sent to defend it. We cannot verify how he disappeared or where he disappeared to, however the Chichen are speculating that he was jumping between this world and the spirit world."

This was an interesting development. The boy had similar powers to that of her son, his uncle. "There's clearly a link," she spoke aloud without realising.

"What do you mean?" The man was on her instantly, speaking quickly this time as he tried to gather as much information as he could.

"Leave me!", She ordered, realising that she had said too much already. It was no coincidence that both her son and the boy had a similar link to the spirit world, they were bound by a blood link.

Maybe it wasn't being born in the spirit world that gave him his powers The voice communicated with her once more. *Perhaps there is a hidden power within your blood line.*

"Perhaps there is" She spoke out loud as if responding to the voice. This was another thing that she hadn't calculated, but it got her thinking.

What if that power flows within us? She began smiling to herself at the prospect they would be truly powerful if she could. The boy was still an obstacle, and they needed to come up with a plan to deal with him before he ruined everything.

Stick to our plan and destroy everything the boy holds dear. She turned to face the flames once more; the warmth kissing her face. Her loose smile morphed into a sinister grin.

Then kill him.

Chapter 21

It was late, dark and windy, Everett hadn't driven in these conditions before. She had gotten into her car rather impulsively, her heart unable to take the pain that she had been feeling any longer. Gripping the steering wheel tightly, she took a deep breath; she needed to get out despite how late it was. She needed to clear her head.

Everyone was now away for the flower war, each having their own part to play, however Everett had not been invited to help the Almec. It was because of her they had lost the dagger. It was because of her that Otto was now under the control of another person.

She adjusted her rearview mirror and could see tears forming at the base of her eyes. The streaming tears shined as a car drove past and the headlights caught her face. Everett brought a hand up to her face to wipe them away before sniffing loudly and taking another deep breath.

If only I hadn't lost my temper, Otto would still be with us she thought to herself as she started up her car. Everett's Dad had always warned her not to drive if she was upset or angry, but she needed to get out for a while, as she couldn't sleep. She did not know where she was going to drive, but she needed an escape from her mind. She would be back shortly and hopefully then she could sleep.

After starting the car up, she gave it a minute to let the heaters kick in so that her windows didn't mist up, and then she set off down the road.

Her mind kept rushing back to Otto and him being under control of another. She didn't deserve to wield his dagger after what she did. Her thoughts were taken back to the look that Otto had given her when she compelled him to attack Arnold's Grandma. She made him do it even though he didn't want to. She did the very thing that she had promised him she would never do, and she had felt terrible ever since.

Kaliska had gone ballistic when Marrok briefed her on what had happened. She has a bigger plan for Otto and him being under control from someone as dangerous as Arnold's Grandma was not part of it. Everett understood why she had then told her not to go with the Almec to the flower war. Even though it hurt being cast aside, Everett felt she deserved it.

The streets were quieter given how late it was, but the roads were passing in a blur as Everett's thoughts continued to go over everything that had played out.

She had driven up past the park and was heading to the tops where she could drive on the winding roads up there. Sitting in the clouds was what she needed right now. Maybe up there she could think more clearly.

"Come on, come on." She impatiently muttered, at a car in front of her, slowing down. She felt apprehensive at the situation, but right now she just wanted to say her piece, to tell everyone how sorry she was. To see Otto back with the Almec and make amends for all of this. The whole situation had gotten out of hand and she just needed to tell them how much they meant to her and that she would do anything she could to make things better, to make things go back to how they were. She raised her hand to the column where her stereo was and pressed to make a call. Scrolling through the names, she stopped at Arnold before pressing for her bluetooth to ring him.

She paused for a moment before hitting dial, her chest pounding with nerves as the phone rang out. They had broken up, but right now, he was the only person she could speak to about how she was feeling. He had always been there for her, although even he might not want to speak with her after how she had been with him. Somehow, in the matter of a week, she had lost everyone that she held dear.

To her frustration, the phone continued to ring and ring with no answer.

"Hi it's Arnold lease leave a message after the beep," His voice prompted, not helping with the already stressful situation.

Everett paused, not knowing what to say, confused about her thoughts and feelings. Not wanting to hurt anyone, but needing to explain why she was calling so late.

"It's me." She started hesitantly. "Sorry for calling you so late but I need to talk to someone about everything that's happened."

There was a bang and Everett's heart raced. Losing control of her car, she felt it pull to the side in an instant. Everett's heart raced as she gripped the steering wheel tightly as she fought to keep the car under control. Everything happened in a blur, Everett had completely lost control of the car. It hurtled to the side and raised onto the curb and across the road. The car stopped as it wrapped itself around the corner of a boundary wall to one of the derelict factories, earmarked to be demolished later that year. There was a loud smash as she collided, then there was nothing. A silence that could send a shiver down anyone's spine.

The car rolled backwards slowly, before stopping on the path. Everett sat motionless in the driver's seat, blood trickling from her ear.

A slender figure stepped out from the shadows from across the road and walked towards the car, her heels echoing on the street. She knew she needed to be fast, as there was only a matter of time before people came from their houses to see what had happened. She moved quickly to the back wheel of the car where she removed the small blade she had thrown from the back tyre of the wreckage.

Hearing a door behind her, she called out delicately to the old man who had come to his door to see what had happened. He was wearing his nightclothes and was blinking wildly from being startled awake. "Quick, someone ring an ambulance." She called out, feigning concern.

The man turned and headed back inside to get help; she hadn't wanted to be seen, but then again, it was not like anyone would recognise her.

She strolled towards the front of the vehicle with her feigned concern, putting on a show for anyone that may come out. This was all part of the plan.

They just wanted to hurt Arnold and what better way than this. After all these were the only people within the Chichen that knew that she existed. It would not be long now before the entire world knew of her existence. It would not be long now until she removed the Chichen from power and took control for herself.

The broken glass crunched under her feet as she patrolled the car. She felt satisfied with the carnage, the twisted metal showing off the heavy impact she had hoped for.

"You will be ok, sweetheart." She continued to pretend as though she was helping, her soft voice reassuring. Her words were a lie. Her intention was to make sure that she did not make it from the wreckage alive. She reached in and brushed back Everett's hair. Everett wasn't responsive to her touch. She could see through the windows that others were now heading to the car to help, her face contorted as she spoke in Everett's ear. "You think you can try to kill us and nothing happen to you," she hissed venomously before stepping away from the car and let the people arriving try to save her. "She's not moving, someone help her." She pretended to be hysterical as a middle-aged woman rushed past to help.

"It's ok I am a nurse," she explained as she leant into the car. "Can you hear me?" She began talking to Everett as she assessed her condition.

Muttered words formed as the crowd grew to see what had happened. It was at this point that she took her opportunity to leave and she faded into the shadows as the loud sirens of the ambulance rang out in the distance.

She deserves this

Chapter 22

There was a loud bang on the door, which snapped Arnold out of his deep sleep. There was another bang on the door, followed by another and another, each time getting more and more frantic.

"I'm coming!" Arnold snapped; his head groggy from the sudden awakening.

"It's George, Arnold please open up." Her voice called back, frantic and broken. She continued to knock, despite Arnold calling out again that he was on his way.

He reached for the door, releasing the latch and pulling it open.

George stood in the hallway. She was shaking uncontrollably, still in her pyjamas. Her hair ruffled, her eyes bright pink and puffy. Her breathing was fast and Arnold wondered if she was having a panic attack.

"What's going on?" Arnold panicked. He had never seen George this inconsolable.

Her face was blemished, her cheeks blotchy. She entered Arnold's room and tried to speak. "E, Ev, Ever" she started, but she couldn't form her words as she tried to talk to Arnold.

"Hey, hey, hey," Arnold rushed towards her and placed both his hands on George's arms and stared deep into her eyes. "You need to breathe George, listen to my voice."

George continued to breathe erratically, unable to control herself.

"George, listen to me. You are going to pass out if you don't listen."

George tried to push Arnold away. He recognised the need to escape, the claustrophobic feeling but he stood firm and continued to talk to her as he tried to help.

"Breathe with me," Arnold directed, and he breathed in and out slowly, hoping that George would copy. To his relief, she did and although her breathing was erratic, she could bring this under better control.

After a minute George had composed herself enough to speak, although the tears had yet to stop falling.

"What is it, George?" Arnold asked delicately. "Talk to me, I can't help if you don't tell me."

George looked pained as her green eyes fixed on Arnold's. Her words still trapped in her throat, as if whatever she needed to say was too painful.

"It's Everett," she explained.

"What about her?" Arnold's mind raced, given the state that George had turned up to his room in.

George took another deep breath and composed herself, but not much before continuing. "She's crashed her car."

Arnold worried. He could feel the colour drain from him as George spoke. Suddenly his legs felt heavy, as if they were made of stone, but he kept himself standing. "When? How? Is she ok?" He pressed, needing an answer.

George didn't reply as she struggled to form the words, looking to the floor for comfort, unable to look Arnold in the eye.

"GEORGE!" Arnold snapped at her.

"NO!" George shouted back. "No, she's not ok Arnold." George burst into tears again, her words getting stuck once more. "She didn't make it, she's gone."

George's words hit Arnold like a sledgehammer. He rushed to George as her own legs gave way and caught her. He hugged her as tightly as he could as she started crying uncontrollably into his chest. His own tears fell down his face as his chest beat harshly. He wanted the ground to swallow him up; he wanted someone to wake him and tell him that this was all just a nightmare.

Everett was gone, and she was never coming back. He would never see her ice-blue eyes, or listen to her talk. In an instant, it was all gone. She had been taken from this earth with no warning. The two continued to cry together. Arnold not knowing what to say, simply continued to hug George whilst she did the same to him.

The warmth hit him first, then he felt the strange pull in his stomach.

"Not now!" Arnold cursed. Now wasn't the time for this.

George looked at Arnold with a puzzled expression.

"It's happening George, I can't always control this." Arnold let go of George as he tried in vain to prevent it from happening.

The room whirled around him. George soon became a blur, the pink of her pyjamas blending with the grey colours from the walls within his room. Everything continued to spin until nothing was recognisable and Arnold was overcome with dizziness until he could not stand any longer. His legs gave way suddenly and he slammed against the ground. In an instant, everything stopped spinning around him and he took a deep breath of the thickened air. The warmth rose up within him and turned into a hot flush. Arnold planted his hands on the floor before vomiting. As transitions to the spirit world go, that had been the worst one he had experienced yet.

"What brings you here?" Levent's voice asked, intrigued.

Arnold was just as surprised as Levent. They had been training in the dreamscape, but he had never actually been in the spirit world with him. "How are you here?" Arnold asked as he wiped his mouth.

"I come here at night when the guards won't see, in between checks. I don't stay for long. It seems you have transported here like I can. Your powers certainly are strong, boy." Levent's eyes widened at the realisation of Arnold's ever developing powers and abilities. "Interesting indeed." Levent cast his eyes over Arnold before noticing the tears in his eyes. "What's wrong? What's happened?" He asked.

"It's Everett, she has been in an accident." Arnold stuttered, just like George had when she had been telling him. :She's dead, Levent. Everett is dead." Arnold dropped back to his knees and cried once more, his tears splashing onto the dirt where he knelt.

Levent stopped his meditation and stood up to offer a hand to Arnold, "Listen boy, you need to control your emotions and quickly." He cut a concerned figure. "What you are feeling now, that hurt, that pain. That is exactly what I went through when Kaliska was murdered." He paused for a moment before correcting himself "When I thought Kaliska had been murdered. The emotions you are feeling right now, you need to suppress them. Otherwise, I fear you may end up trapped here like I once was."

"It's not like I can just switch them off," Arnold snapped, frustrated at the advice that Levent was giving him.

"That's not what I am asking you to do, if you would just listen." Levent spoke through gritted teeth, frustrated at Arnold's response to him. "If we do not get you back now, then you may end up here for a long time. Do you want to end up like me?"

"Sorry." Arnold couldn't believe he was apologising to him, but felt it was the right thing to do. He closed his eyes and focused his mind. Memories that he shared with Everett began flashing into his mind. As much as he tried not to think about her because of the pain, the memories came thick and fast. The time they had spent together.

"Focus Arnold," Levent cut off Arnold's thoughts, "You need to focus on your anchor; focus on your Mum and Dad,"

Arnold remembered what Levent had told him and thought of his Mum and Dad, the worry they would go through if he was to go missing due to him being stuck in the spirit world. They would be in a pain even worse than what he was feeling now and he would hate for them to experience it. As he would do when spirit walking, he thought about them both until he felt the tug in his stomach. He opened his eyes. "I'm anchored," he explained to Levent.

"Good, the last thing you need is to be stuck here. You need to get back, Arnold. I am sorry about Everett, I truly am."

With that, Levent blurred into the surroundings as the world spun around him once more. It wasn't long before Arnold felt the carpeted floor of his room as he came back to this world with a thud.

"Arnold, Arnold!" George spoke in a worried tone.

As Arnold waited for the room to stop spinning, George helped him to his feet. "How long was I gone?"

"A few seconds. Not long at all," George replied, "I thought you were getting control of your spirit walking."

"That wasn't spirit walking," Arnold explained. "I don't know what that was, but I am glad to be back." He reached forward and took hold of George to hug her again. "If I lose control, I might not be able to get back."

"How do you know?" Her breathing stifled as she sniffed up her tears.

"That doesn't matter. All that does matter is that we are here for each other." Arnold's phone lit up behind him and vibrated loudly with a reminder. Moving away from George, he picked it up to see a missed call from Everett.

"I've a missed call from her." His heart sank. When had Everett called him? Would her accident have happened if he had picked up? Why did he have to be in such a deep sleep? His hand started shaking straight away to a point where he was only just able to keep hold of the phone. Glancing at the top of the screen, he noticed the symbol for a voicemail. Saying nothing, he pressed on the icon before bringing his phone up to his ear.

"Hi it's me, Sorry for calling you so late but I need to talk to someone about everything that's happened" It was Everett, it was almost too much for Arnold as her soft voice came through it was like she was talking to him from the heavens.

Then came the ear-splitting noise of her car crashing as she lost control of the vehicle. Arnold's shaking became worse, he could not believe what he was listening to. Then nothing for a moment. An eery silence and the clicking sound of something which Arnold assumed was her indicator. It was too much for him. Arnold thought he was going to be sick. He had just heard the crash that had killed her.

As he was about to hang up, Arnold heard the crunching

sound of glass and thought that it was Everett struggling to move.

Then came another voice.

"You will be ok sweetheart," The woman's voice didn't appear distinct and at first it appeared it was a passer-by come to help Everett. That was, until the next words were spoken. Words that turned Arnold's blood cold in an instant. "You think you can try to kill us and nothing happen to you." Her words were callous and cold.

It was a coldness that Arnold recognised as his Grandma's straight away.

"She did this!" Arnold was furious. "It was my Grandma!"

"What do you mean? How do you know?" George was confused, but Arnold didn't have time to explain.

"I am going to kill her for what she has done!" His body had tensed up, and he was squeezing his phone now. He moved to the door to exit. He did not know where she was, but he was determined to find her.

"Woah, you can't go anywhere like that Arnold," George pressed her hands against him to stop him leaving. "Arnold don't react like this. If it was her, then this is how she will want you to react."

Arnold paused for a moment and thought about it. Maybe that was his Grandma's plan after all. If he went too far, he would be thrown out of the Chichen for sure or even locked away. He had the evidence he needed, and he was determined that he was going to take her down. She would pay for what she had done to Everett, and Arnold would not stop until she did.

It had been the longest night of Arnold's life; he had barely slept. All he could think about was Everett. George had stayed in his room with him and was curled up next to him on his bed. She was so quiet when asleep that at times Arnold wondered if she was even breathing.

It had taken a long time for George to fall asleep, but the two of them had sat talking about Everett for a couple of hours, crying together and sharing memories until eventually George had drifted off. It was an escape that Arnold wished he could have himself, his mind was racing. It still didn't seem real that this was all happening, that Everett was gone. Arnold's eyes welled for what felt like the thousandth time as he thought about her. Arnold's alarm set off, he had set it for seven to get ready for whatever was in store for him today. His body still ached from the previous day, even more than it should, given that he had hardly rested before George had come with the news about Everett.

The room was silent aside from the nature that was already awake outside; it felt calm and peaceful. Arnold wished they could just go back to when they were at school and all he needed to worry about was getting through the school day. So much had happened since then. It had been nothing short of a whirlwind since Arnold joined the Chichen, since he undertook his ch'ahb'. Levent, Otto, the coal mines, his Grandad, the Almec. There had been so much that had happened to him over the last couple of years. He wished they could go back even only one day so that Everett may still be here. George stirred because of the alarm and looked up at Arnold through blinkered eyes. She was barely recognisable without her beanie hat on.

"Hey," she croaked.

Arnold shuffled down, so that he was level with her, and the two looked into each other's eyes. "Hey," Arnold smiled back at her. He just wanted George to feel a little better. After all, she had just lost her best friend.

"I can't promise you that everything is going to be ok George, I wish I could. I am going to make sure that she pays for what she has done." Arnold explained.

"I know, just make sure you don't lose yourself in the process. That is what she will be trying to do." George dragged herself out of bed and stretched as hard as she could, her back clicking as she did. "I best get ready, too. I need to speak to Marrok and the Almec about what has happened." With this she made to the door, her face still a picture of sadness.

Arnold wished he could take her pain away, but he couldn't. All he could do now was see that justice was done.

By nine o'clock Arnold had been for a run, showered, dressed and had breakfast. He headed down to the hall room as he had been instructed the night before. As he entered, the room seemed to fall silent. Mr Whittaker sat with Miss Stone and some other Elders at the top of the room. The hall was ornately decorated, the different banners of the Chichen, the Almec and the Calmecac hung from the ceiling in varying colours. The room was filled with chairs on each side, which reminded Arnold of a wedding ceremony. Mr Whittaker looked towards Arnold and stopped whatever it was he was saying to the Grand Elder. He left the table where they sat and moved towards Arnold quickly.

"Ethon, what is the meaning of this?" Mr Whittaker was already dressed in his ceremonial robes. They were a deep purple colour, his sleeves decorated with the various stripes and badges he had earned as a Doyen and as that as an Elder. "You were instructed to be here for half-past nine and to be wearing your armour." Mr Whittaker did not seem impressed with Arnold.

"Sir, I need to speak to you," Arnold started.

Mr Whittaker cut him off by raising a hand, "Is this about your friend?" He started. "I was told about the accident last night. I am sorry to hear about her." Mr Whittaker appeared genuine in what he was saying, but appeared somewhat disinterested in the situation.

"Sir, it wasn't an accident." Arnold jumped in. "Someone created the accident, I have the evidence on my phone." He took out his phone from his pocket and accessed his voicemail to show Mr Whittaker. "It was her, it was my Grandma."

"Is everything ok?" Miss Stone's voice called out as she approached the two of them. 'The main part of the flower war is due to start and all I see is our contender still unprepared for his duties." She cast her eyes over Arnold and gave him a disapproving look. "You can't let things that happen outside of here affect your concentration. There is too much at stake."

Arnold was shocked by her cold response. If Mr Whittaker knew what had happened to Everett, then Miss Stone would too, and the way that she had referred to her death so flippantly angered him.

"Ethon was telling me he doesn't believe the car crash which involved his friend was an accident." Mr Whittaker began explaining. "He says he has evidence that proves it was his Grandma."

Miss Stone's nostrils flared at the mention of her, "That woman," She scowled at Arnold, who was fumbling with his phone. "How do you intend on proving it?"

He passed his phone to Miss Stone, who placed this against her ear and listened to the voicemail. After it had finished playing, she handed it back over to Arnold. "That evidence will never hold up. It is barely audible. How can you be sure?"

"I just know." Arnold replied curtly.

"Unfortunately, that is not good enough. I am sorry for your friend Arnold. I really am, but you need to focus on today. As I have said, there is too much at stake." As sincere as Mr Whittaker had seemed when offering Arnold his condolences, Miss Stone did not.

Arnold felt as though his blood was about to boil and clenched his jaw tightly in frustration. "Is that it, then? Is that all Everett gets? Treated as an inconvenience and brushed to the side like she doesn't matter." His voice raised, his words echoed around the hall. People began looking over to see what all the commotion was.

"I suggest you lower your voice and remember who you are addressing." Miss Stone challenged Arnold, her words crisp and sharp.

"You care more for the respect you command because of your rank than you do for justice being done. I couldn't care less about who I am addressing!" Arnold was furious and in utter disbelief at the response he was getting.

"I care about the fate of the Chichen. We don't want the power of the country falling into another's hand." Miss Stone was equally furious at Arnold. "May I suggest you escort Master Ethon back to his room to ready himself for today's challenge." Miss Stone stared at Mr Whittaker momentarily before turning on her heels and heading back to her table.

"Don't worry sir, I can escort myself.' Arnold feigned a bow to Mr Whittaker before turning to leave. Arnold had not expected that response in a million years. The Chichen didn't care about the crime that had been committed. All they cared about was holding onto the power that they had. Arnold was walking fast to escape the hall. He glanced up to see the emblem of his

Chichen, a rose with a bee sat within it and for a moment he contemplated reaching for it and dragging it down from the walls.

"Arnold." A voice called over from the entrance way.

It was Kaliska, ready for the day's challenge. She was already in her bone mail armour. Arnold knew it was bone mail, as Marrok had previously explained this to him. In the Almec, part of their initiation into adulthood involved crafting their own armour. They would use the consecrated bones of the spirit beast they were bound to. This intensified their connection to the spirit world and enhanced their abilities when wearing the armour. Kaliska's armour was more refined than what Arnold had previously seen Marrok wearing. It was neater and appeared more intricate. Bits of bone connected to form panels across Kaliska's chest, arms and legs. Underneath the armour, Kaliska only wore clothes to protect her modesty. Arnold couldn't help but think that her armour would grant her greater agility and movement, but the gaps between panels would leave her vulnerable. She also wore a large headdress with the hyde of her spirit beast cast over her shoulders as if the animal was taking a large bite out of her head. It looked wolf like, but Arnold could not tell what animal it was.

"It's a coyote," Kaliska smiled softly at Arnold. 'Arnold, I am so sorry to hear about Everett.' Her words were genuine. She stepped to Arnold without hesitation and wrapped her arms around him, hugging him tightly. The bone armour felt uncomfortable against him, but it was the maternal embrace he needed to comfort him. It took everything Arnold had not to burst into tears, but he held them back, not wishing to return to the spirit world.

"Thank you, I can't believe she is gone,"

"She still lives on in all of you, don't let her memory fade and she will always be around," Kaliska smiled at Arnold before stepping away from him. "Are you ready for today?"

Arnold shook his head. He had given the day little thought and felt completely unprepared given everything that had happened. After the conversation he just had with the grand elder, he also felt disillusioned. "Why are we doing this, Kaliska?"

"That is a good question Arnold, factions enter the flower war as a way of obtaining power, to rule over the lands. This is how it has been for as long as time can tell."

"What do you want?" Arnold asked.

"A voice. I don't want power for my people, I just want them to have a voice. For too long have we remained silent, standing by as the Chichen grow stronger and stronger. Unable to do anything as they take sacred artefacts that do not belong to them. All because they fear the power that this can grant menials. People should have access to artefacts if they prove themselves. It is the only way they activate. In the Almec, we gift artefacts to those who are not blessed with a spirit beast to enable them." Kaliska spoke with compassion, something Arnold felt the Chichen lacked. He had so many questions he wanted to ask, but he knew he didn't have long to get changed into his armour.

"Where's Marrok?" Arnold asked, realising he was not at his mother's side.

"He is comforting George and recovering from yesterday. He was part of the team I put together to protect Valin's armour."

"I don't know if I should tell you this, but Levent knows about Marrok." Arnold spoke quickly, wanting to explain before he ran out of time.

193

"Levent is not the man I thought he was. He has walked a dark path for too long to play any part in our son's life." Kaliska confirmed Arnold's theory about Levent and Marrok.

"What if he only walked that path because he thought the Chichen had murdered you?" Arnold couldn't believe that he was actually fighting Levent's corner on this one.

"Then I would say that you have been spending too much time with him Arnold. There is no absolution for the crimes he has committed. Need I remind you of your grandfather?" Kaliska's demeanor changed in an instant, she was frustrated with Arnold.

Arnold felt a pang of guilt. Had he brought dishonour in working with Levent, even if it was the only way for him to control his abilities. Surely his Grandad would understand this.

"I have done what I have needed to in order to control my abilities,' Arnold tried to explain, 'I won't apologise for that."

"Be careful Arnold, or you will end up like him. Do not trust the words that he speaks to you. If Levent is helping you, then there will be a reason for it."

Kaliska nodded towards Arnold and headed to the hall. "Good luck today Arnold, I wish you safe passage through this war." With this, Kaliska disappeared out of sight.

Arnold left the reception area to head back to his room. He needed to get changed and ready for whatever challenge was awaiting him today.

Chapter 23

Arnold stood staring into the full-length mirror in his room. He was in his armour. He just wanted to look it over before he left. It felt weightless to wear, no different from wearing a pair of jeans and a t-shirt. The feathers that covered the armour looked like it was cast into the armour to create the panels, like they were bound together somehow to create a unique style of chain-mail. He felt no different for wearing it. In all honestly, he felt he looked a little ridiculous wearing such ancient armour. Still traditions were traditions and Arnold needed to abide by these in order to bring honour to his family.

All that was left was to put on his helmet. Equally flamboyant as it was impressive, he placed the last piece of armour over his head. It didn't obscure his view as much as he had thought it would, but from inside it was from above where he felt he had a bit of a blind spot. The large beak that protruded from above seemed the least practical part, but Arnold accepted it as part of the completed set.

There was a loud knock at the door, followed quickly by another.

"Ethon, you are going to be late." It was Mr Whittaker. "I am here to escort you to the final challenge."

Mr Whittaker was the last person who Arnold wanted to see

right now and he reluctantly opened the door to him.

"At least you are in your armour," He spoke with a sarcastic tone. Humour did not suit him, and Mr Whittaker looked just as uncomfortable with the situation as Arnold was.

"Nearly didn't bother," Arnold muttered.

"You have no option but to fight today. If you don't, the Chichen would be out of the flower war."

"I know that!" Arnold spat. He wasn't in the mood for Mr Whittaker.

"You need to come with me," Mr Whittaker ignored Arnold's petulance, a rare thing indeed.

"Where are we going?" Arnold quizzed, "What's today's challenge?"

"A three-way duel," Mr Whittaker explained. "I am here to take you to where you will fight the other champions. Whoever wins, will win the contest."

"Already?" Arnold felt surprised that it was already the last challenge.

"There's no need to draw this out longer than it needs to be Ethon. Now please follow me and I will take you down to the arena."

Arena

Arnold had seen nothing that looked anything like an arena while he was exploring the ornamental gardens yesterday. Given the size of the place, it didn't surprise him that there was a hidden arena somewhere inside.

Arnold followed Mr Whittaker out of his room and towards the entrance to the ornamental gardens. In the reception area, Doyen's and Elders lined the walls waiting to greet their champion. Different coloured robes and flags carrying the different crests of the regional Chichens were on full display, like a peacock displaying its feathers. Whereas Arnold appreciated the support and the fact that people had turned up to wish him well, he couldn't help but harbour resentment towards the Chichen. A young woman stood towards the door, her blonde fringe hanging from the front. She smiled at Arnold as he reached the bottom of the stairs and clapped. It wasn't long before the rest of the room followed suit and a raucous applause broke out amongst the small crowd. They wooped and cheered Arnold as he made his exit and began his journey to the arena where he would face his next challenge. The applause and cheers lifted Arnold's spirits slightly as he made it out into the the grounds. To his right were the overgrown hills of the pike, where the ornamental gardens lay hidden from the world. The trees danced with the cool breeze, with the clouds sitting low, the top of the hillside barely visible.

Mr Whittaker walked ahead, the hood on his tunic raised, the base of it trailing along the ground like a bride's dress. However impressive the ceremonial clothes of the Chichen were they seemed impracticable. As they reached the base of the pike, Arnold took a deep breath and focused himself for the task ahead of him and he entered the woodlands. The outside world soon disappeared as they navigated the familiar winding paths that Arnold knew the day before until Mr Whittaker took a sharp left turn off the track. This caught Arnold by surprise, but he quickly followed into the trees and began a steady incline towards another path that the greenery had hidden. There had been a light rain the night before, turning the soil into mud. Arnold found it hard to keep his footing as he continued to follow Mr Whittaker. Reaching for a trailing branch, Arnold only just stopped himself from tumbling backwards down the slope.

What kind of champion would I look like if I arrived covered in mud and dirt he wondered. Even though he had already proven himself capable of fighting in the flower war, he felt that he still had a lot to prove and knew there would still be plenty of people that would expect him to fail.

"This new ability of yours. How did you come about it?" Mr Whittaker broke the uncomfortable silence, choosing to address the elephant in the room.

It was something that Arnold had expected when he returned successful, he night before, armour in hand. He knew that there would have been eyes watching and that the Chichen would know of his hidden abilities; he had braced himself for the interrogation. But it never came. He was allowed to enjoy a drink and some food on his return before being allowed to retire to his room to have a bath and rest.

"It just kind of happened?" Arnold responded quickly, almost defensively. "I had a panic attack and ended up in the spirit world. I call it spirit walking."

"Can you open portals like Levent?" Mr Whittaker fired quickly into the next question without hesitation. 'He has that ability, does he not.' His raised hood dampened Mr Whittaker's words, making it harder for Arnold to hear him over the rustling of the leaves.

"No, I am not like him." Arnold said defensively. "I can't teleport like he can, at least I don't think I can. When I spirit walk, I stay in the same place, just in the spirit world. I can move to another area and reappear in this world at that point." Arnold grabbed hold of another low-hanging branch to stop himself from slipping backwards.

"This is concerning," Mr Whittaker exhaled.

"What do you mean?" asked Arnold.

"You're dabbling in powers and energy that should not be messed with Ethon." Mr Whittaker spoke sharply. "It is not natural to step foot on the plains of the spirit world."

"Says who?" Arnold challenged, just as sharp as Mr Whittaker.

"Says the Elder council Arnold. It's a power too strong. It isn't natural to channel that amount of energy. Imagine what could happen if that kind of power fell into the wrong hands." He began explaining as the two of them reached a clearing and finally some flat ground.

"Who are we to decide who should and shouldn't have this power, though?"

Mr Whittaker turned to face Arnold and looked him deep in his eyes. "We need to keep people safe. We need to stop powers like yours being known about. That way, people will not try to harness raw energy. It would be catastrophic."

"Then what about me? What happens to me when the flower war is over?" Arnold was growing more frustrated now.

"The Elder council is undecided. Some fear the abilities you wield, some feel that you should have your connection to the spirit world severed." He looked pensive as he explained the elder council's stance.

"Severed!? They would have me a menial to keep me under control?" Arnold felt as though his head might pop as his anger rose up inside him. The Elder council would rather strip him of his auro than understand the connection to the spirit world which he held. His mind went back to his Grandad's journal. He had wrote how he had trapped his Grandma in the spirit world for fear of what the Chichen would do to her if they found out about her spirit beast being a dragon. What else would they have done to her other than sever her connection to the spirit world?

"What would have happened if the Chichen had found out about my Grandma? You know, before my Grandad trapped her in the spirit world."

"Ethon, we are nearly there. Need you keep asking questions you know you will not like the answer to?" Mr Whittaker was growing inpatient with Arnold as he turned to continue the walk down the overgrown path.

"Answer me!" Arnold bellowed, "What would they have done to her?"

The tired Elder stopped in his tracks, incensed by how he was being spoken to. "Need I remind you who you are addressing, Ethon?"

"Need I remind you? I am representing the Chichen, putting my life on the line for us." His throat felt hoarse as he almost growled in frustration. "From where I am standing, I am finding it hard to understand what I am fighting for." He paused for a moment, "Sir." He clenched his teeth as he sarcastically ended his sentence. "Either you tell me what they would have done to her, or I will not set one foot in that arena."

Mr Whittaker stared at Arnold for a moment before letting out a sigh large enough to blow over the nearby trees. He was clearly exasperated with Arnold and for a moment, Arnold wondered whether Mr Whittaker would drag Arnold to the arena kicking and screaming. "Ethon, we do not have time for this." Knowing how stubborn Arnold could be, Mr Whittaker gave a look which suggested to Arnold that he realised he would not win this one. "They would have severed her connection," He started "The dragon spirit beast is too dangerous, so many people have died from the chaos that they reap on this world."

Arnold knew there was more. His Grandad would have welcomed her connection being severed. There was no way he would have done what he did, there had to be more. "What else, what else would they have done to her?"

"She is a dangerous woman Arnold, her spirit beast has corrupted her. Look at what she has done in just a short period; attacked the council, triggered the flower war. Killed Everett."

"Don't use her to escape my question." Arnold had to push back his anger. He felt like swinging for Mr Whittaker for the way he was using Everett's death to hide from his answer. "It was only a short time ago that I said I had evidence and you and Miss Stone wouldn't entertain it. Now answer my question."

"They would have executed her. She is corrupted. Even with her connection to the spirit word severed, her mind would still be too warped by the corruption. There's no way to get around it other than death."

Arnold had the response that he had desired, but it was not the answer that he wanted. He felt even more disillusioned about the Chichen. All that time she had spent in the spirit world, however terrible that may have been, at least she was alive. His Grandad had done what he believed he needed to do to save her. If death awaited her, he really had no choice.

No wonder she hates them Arnold thought to himself.

"The reason she is so warped is because of the Chichen. Everything she has experienced is because of them."

"Don't you mean us Ethon, remember you are part of the Chichen." Mr Whittaker corrected him. "It corrupted her long before now Arnold, you only need to look at your Grandma to understand how unnatural she is. She must be at least seventy years old, yet she has the appearance of someone in their twenties. The arena is just here, we don't have time Ethon, I will answer any other questions you have after you are done here." Mr Whittaker gestured to up the path.

Arnold pressed forward, albeit reluctantly. He was fizzing inside. His Grandma was not innocent, he wasn't naive enough to believe this. He was however, and mostly, the Elder council were potentially going to treat him like her all because he had abilities they are afraid of.

"Just continue up the path and you will see where we need to go." Mr Whittaker followed from behind this time, to keep Arnold on track and not allow any more delays.

Arnold continued to trudge along the path as directed, any semblance of motivation long gone. Soon he would have to face Kaliska and Valin in a three-way battle. It wasn't long before the trees opened up to reveal a huge open space. The stone walled arena sat in the middle. It was like nothing Arnold had seen before.

Arnold thought of the kind of Colosseum that you would see in Rome. But this arena was built into the ground, the open top drew level with the ground. It was oval and in good condition, given the age of the structure. There was a large group of people gathered on the outside. Using his enhanced vision, Arnold could see the differing-coloured robes from those within the Chichen, as well as members of the Almec. They were easy to spot because of the bone mail armour they wore with the animal head dresses. Arnold quickly spotted Marrok. One of his eyes were bruised and swollen shut from his attempt at stopping Valin.

To the right of this group stood a hand full of people wearing the hides of animals as their armour. Arnold knew that these were of the Calmecac in an instance. Four of the people stood there were the ones that had tried to kill Arnold the day before. They looked nervous and were smarting from the injuries they had sustained. To the right of them Arnold could see his Grandma, to her left stood a vacant Otto, his eyes glazed over. A sign he was under the control of his dagger.

A rush of blood coursed through Arnold, and he set off, walking at pace towards his Grandma. He wanted to bring her to justice for what she had done to Everett. She was a murderer. Even if the Chichen wouldn't do anything about it, Arnold would. He wasn't scared of her like the Elder council was. As he moved forward, he found himself suddenly stopped. A hand gripped his arm like a vice, stopping him in his tracks.

"Let me go!" Arnold spat. He could feel the power in the grip and tried to break free.

Mr Whittaker was not allowing this behavior. "Calm yourself, Ethon, do not do anything brash." He was stony faced, his eyes switched from Arnold to his Grandma and back again. "This is the reaction she wants, do you not think this? She wants you to lose your head, to hinder your chances of winning. You need to think with this instead of this." Mr Whittaker put his finger to Arnold's head, followed by his heart. "You fight with heart, Ethon, but that will only get you so far. If you don't start fighting with your brain, you will find that you will not last long in combat." He gave Arnold a death stare before letting go of his arm.

Arnold pulled his arm away petulantly and stared back at Mr Whittaker. He was powerful, Arnold thought that Mr Whittaker was harsh in training. If his grip was anything to go by, it was in fact the opposite; he had been going easy on him all this time.

"Keep your head, trust me if she is responsible for Everett's death, she will face justice."

Composing himself, Arnold continued across the opening until he reached the top of the arena where the larger group stood.

"Here he is, here is our champion," It was Miss Stone, she was addressing the Elder council that had gathered. She smiled at Arnold as they approached, reaching her arm out to usher him towards their group. She was very different from the harsh woman he had spoken with earlier in the day. Was it all an act. Her niceties seemed too exaggerated, too over the top to be real. One thing that Arnold knew was that he didn't trust her, not one bit.

Arnold didn't acknowledge her as he was surrounded by the members of the elder council, their coloured robes making Arnold feel like he had been engulfed by a rainbow. Hands patted him, voices spoke, wishing him luck and favour from the gods.

"Let the boy breathe," Miss Stone directed and the group widened around him, giving him a bit more space. "Our champion wears his sacred armour ready for battle; ready to represent our ancient ways, our ancient traditions." The crowd grew silent as Miss Stone spoke. "He puts his life on the line for the Chichen, yes it was his father who was selected, but because of his blood link, he has taken his place. Despite the risk to his own life, he stands before us, ready to risk it all to protect our ways. For that Arnold, I commend you." There was a cheer from within the group that slowly echoed outwards as the others joined in with fractious approval.

"Across there stands an abomination, a woman corrupted by the dragon spirit beast inside her." The group jeered at the mention of Arnold's Grandma. "She hides behind ancient laws that bind us from apprehending her, through triggering the flower war she is protected. Once this is through though, when our champion stands victorious on the battlefield." Miss Stone paused for dramatic effect, to good effect as the Elder council grew more boisterous. "And he will stand victorious," She turned to give Arnold a fake smile, "She will be brought to justice for the things she has done and she will be separated from her spirit beast." The group gave another cheer and began clapping and patting Arnold like a dog as they attempted to rally him for the fight ahead.

Miss Stone's impromptu speech had the opposite effect on Arnold. He hated his Grandma for what she had done, she should be brought to justice and imprisoned. This was the way they had always taught him since joining the Chichen, not severing connections or executing people. Maybe if he won this thing, he would have more sway to insist on her being brought to justice and imprisoned the right way.

"This way Ethon," Mr Whittaker pressed Arnold in the back to move him forward and away from the group.

Arnold shuffled forwards, the arena looked far more intimidating as he drew closer to the entrance. As he reached the top, looking down, he could see cobbled stone steps to the open space where he and the other champions would be pitted against each other. Kaliska was already waiting in the centre of the arena. She sat in the battle gear that Arnold had seen her in earlier. She looked to be meditating, sat on a rock in the corner of the far side of the arena. She looked peaceful and serene, as if the flower war didn't phase her at all. Arnold on the other hand, looked so pale he could have been a ghost. There was an atmosphere as the Almec and Chichen members formed a crowd on the outer edge of the arena above. Their shouts and cries echoing through the arena like a battering ram. The cheers hit Arnold in the chest hard and his heart began beating faster and harder, his adrenaline kicking in as the atmosphere engulfed him like flames on paper.

There was a ruckus as the smallest group moved to fill a gap with their presence, they were far rowdier, far more elated than the other groups and began chanting in unison and banging their hands aggressively against their shields as they drowned out the noise of the Almec and Chichen combined.

"Valin, Valin, Valin!" the group chanted in unison as they awaited their champion to arrive and present himself in the arena.

Arnold's heart was pounding as hard as ever now. He looked above at the baying crowds and could not believe the spectacle that was unfolding. Since when had the flower war become a blood sport? honour and bravery had been cast to the side like rubbish as if they were not important anymore. All the pompous words of valour fading memories in Arnold's mind. He didn't feel desperate to win this contest for the Chichen; he felt desperate to survive.

A low jeer rang out amongst the Calmecac as they roared in unison. Their champion had arrived. The oval walls of the arena must have stood around fifty feet tall. At the top stood the man chosen to represent the Calmecac, Valin. Arnold's vision meant he could see the smug luck on his face as he played up to the baying crowd. His chest was covered in black fur and the chest piece of an animal dried out and hardened to form his battle armour. His legs were uncovered, except for his thighs, that had a similar style of armour bound around them. He wore no helmet. He had a swagger about him, a smugness that irritated Arnold. His face smiling as he laughed and jostled with the other members of the Calmecac. He pretended as though he had lost his balance and feigned stumbling to the edge as if he might fall. His audience lapped it up as they began hooting and laughing.

Valin stared into the void before him for a few seconds.

Suddenly Valin leapt forward from the edge and plummeted like lead to the ground below. He landed in the dirt, a cloud of dust surrounding him as he regained his balance perfectly. He glanced up at Arnold and cut him an arrogant smile.

Arnold had seen nothing like it. He didn't know it was possible to leap such a distance. Judging by the gasps he heard from the Elder council, he quickly realised neither had they.

"It's unnatural," a quivering voice called down into the chasm the three of them found themselves in.

"What powerful magic has she bestowed upon him? This is preposterous!" Another voice boomed.

Valin stood tall and raised his hands to the two hilts that were strapped to his back. He unsheathed his weapons to reveal twin morning stars. The solid metal balls covered in spikes and attached to the end of a metal pole that he gripped tightly. He raised them high as if holding a trophy proudly at a football match. The members of the Calmecac were now at their loudest as they roared with appreciation for him.

Arnold had faced off against Valin previously with Marrok and he had ferociously beaten the two of them, his power as incredible as it was intimidating. If Arnold was going to beat him, he was going to have to fight like he had never had before. He was going to have to dig the deepest he ever had.

Kaliska opened her eyes, unphased by the spectacle that Valin had just put on and stood proudly as she prepared herself. She looked towards Arnold before casting him a nod. Nothing more, nothing less. She was focused and determined.

Arnold felt as though his legs could give way, his armour suddenly feeling heavier than it ever had. This was it. This was everything he had been training for. He could only hope that it would all pay off, that it would all be worthwhile.

"Members of the Chichen, the Almec," Miss Stone paused for a moment awkwardly before reluctantly continuing, "and the Cal-me-cac. Our champions are here. All have passed the initial trials of the flower war and claimed their armour for them all. All that awaits now is for the final trial, trial by combat. The winning champion's faction will take control as dictated by the laws passed down by our ancestors millennia ago."

"We grow tired of your words!" Arnold's Grandma heckled from the other side, breaking her silence like a knife through butter. She stepped towards the edge before casting her eyes down at Valin. "Valin, kill them both." The members of the Calmecac erupted wildly as they celebrated the command, desperate to see what their champion would do to Kaliska and Arnold.

Valin did not wait around for an invitation. Before the battle was declared open, he ran straight towards Kaliska. He raised both morning stars above his head while roaring with aggression and brought them both down on Kaliska. Kaliska remained calm and kicked up her spear that lay on the ground. Arnold hadn't noticed this previously and wondered if Kaliska had hidden this under the dirt. The spear flicked up smoothly from the ground and Kaliska grabbed it before planting the spear in the ground and kicking the bottom. She used the force to build up momentum as she swung her spear above her to parry away Valin's strike before spinning and cracking the side of the pole into his back. With a crack, Valin fired forward, but he spun with a smile on his face and swiped from the side with one of his morning stars. Kaliska blocked this before Valin struck with the other. Kaliska was equally quick to this, spinning her spear to block the attack from the other side.

Arnold stood gawping at the fight in front of him, not knowing what best to do.

Valin continued his volley of attacks, aiming a blow at each side of Kaliska without reprieve. Powerful blows rained from the sides and Kaliska continued to parry each time, needing to move backwards to keep her balance. The Calmecac roared each time Valin's weapons met Kaliska's on the battlefield. The sound of metal on metal ringing out loudly across the arena like violent wind chimes.

With a flick of her spear, Kaliska could force some distance between herself and Valin and buy herself a moment's rest from his attacks. The two stared each other down for a moment, neither shifting their gaze from one another.

Arnold felt like a loose part. The only thing he was certain of was that he didn't want to see any harm come to Kaliska. She had helped his Grandad, Arnold and Otto over the last year and was an excellent leader. As good as she was at leading, it was becoming clear to Arnold that she was even better at combat with a focus on defence.

Valin stepped forward, his stance aggressive and hostile, looking for an opening to strike down Kaliska. Kaliska started glowing a violet colour. It trailed down her spear as she held it out in front of her and began spinning it, the trail formed a glowing figure of eight as she spun it from side to side. The energy she was emitting was powerful, and Valin's hair blew backwards from the force. He simply smiled at the challenge in front of him.

He began swinging his weapons over and over, to no avail. Kaliska continued to block his assault. Each time their weapons met, the power from her weapon pulsated to a point where Arnold could feel the energy hitting him. Steel on steel continued to ring out, the Calmecac continued to cheer each blow. Valin was relentless and continued to strike at Kaliska. His eyes widened with frustration as he attempted to break her defense.

A few more blows and Valin eventually stopped to regain his breath. There was no way he was breaking through. He panted heavily for a moment before switching his gaze to Arnold, pointing his morning star at him and grinning.

"Your next coward," He shouted and smashed his morning star into the ground with force. The mace part broke off before Valin did the same with the other. All he held in his hands was the metal hilt of his weapons.

No, he can't can he? Arnold thought as he wondered what Valin was doing.

Both his hands glowed. His auro was like nothing Arnold had ever seen before. It didn't look natural, like the spirit world energy was being manipulated unnaturally.

Arnold looked up to the skies where his Grandma stood, her calm and steady gaze casting down on the fight below.

Valin's auro continued to glow deep blue, with a lighter blue tone on the inside, similar to what you see within a negative photo.

"Negative energy? What has she done to you?" Arnold muttered to himself as Valin continued to build up his auro. He growled as he focused his energy, his auro engulfed the hilt of his weapon. Valin flicked his wrist as if cracking a whip and a chain formed at the end of the hilts and attached to the end of this was another solid spiked ball, Valin was spirit wielding.

"Are you watching?" He called over to Arnold, taunting him. "Think you are the only one who can spirit wield?"

He spun his glowing weapon above his head, building up

momentum before swinging it wildly at Kaliska. The sound of the energies of the two weapons meeting boomed out, releasing another wave of raw energy across the battlefield.

Valins' weapon bounced off and he swung his left hand to repeat the attack and then again on his right. Kaliska gave a panicked look of surprise at the power Valin was displaying, each time only just managing to keep her defensive stance and her spear spinning. On the fourth blow, Valin's chained morning star wrapped around the shaft of Kaliska's spear like a swing ball. It stopped her momentum in an instance and Valin swung his free weapon at her from her open side. Kaliska grabbed hold of his wrist and pressed back, preventing the attack from connecting with her. The two struggled against one another until Valin threw his head forward and connected with Kaliska's face. Dazed, she staggered backwards before Valin spun and released a powerful kick to her chest, sending her sprawling backwards into the dirt until she slid to a stop.

Valin started spinning his morning stars by his side as he walked towards her slowly. He was playing with her. Whatever his Grandma had done to him, he had become far too strong for Kaliska and most likely Arnold too.

"Arnold, do something!" Marrok called down from the top, pleading for Arnold to help his Mum.

Without hesitation Arnold sprinted forward to do whatever he could to help. As Valin approached Kaliska, he swung both morning stars in tandem until he aimed to bring them down on a defenceless Kaliska. He roared as he sought to bring her life to an end, but his weapon met an equal force which pushed him backwards away from her.

As the dust settled, Valin realised that Arnold had entered the fight, his spirit weapon summoned and gripped tightly in his hands. He was standing in front of Kaliska, having just stopped her life from being brought to a bloodied end.

"Finally decided to join the fight, have we?" Valin growled, he was clearly irked by Arnold's intervention. "You understand that there can only be one winner, don't you?"

"I won't let you kill her," Arnold growled back, concentrating his energy on his machuahuitl as he stood his ground.

"Very well, let's see what you can do!" He swung his morning star at Arnold who knocked it away before aiming a blow at Valin's other hand. He quickly swung the weapon back into Valin's trailing hand before stepping into his personal space and ramming his shoulder into him. The force caused Valin to stumble backwards, his smug grin slowly contorting into frustration.

Kaliska fired past Arnold quickly with her spear pointed at Valin. He attempted to knock this away, but the momentum knocked the morning star out of his right hand. The members of the Almec cheered on their champion as she fought back against the Calmecac. Valin swung down towards Kaliska's spear to knock this away, but Kaliska let the chain wrap around her spear before forcing his other morning star out of his left hand. Arnold followed this up with a powerful kick to his midrif. Valin spluttered and fell backwards into the dirt, turning to his side to catch his breath.

Valin looked up towards Arnold's Grandma, then back towards Arnold making Arnold feel uneasy. It had been too easy to disarm Valin, too easy to knock him down. Arnold had faced Valin before. Something wasn't right here.

Valin flipped back to his feet and growled at both Kaliska and Arnold, his teeth bared, his negative energy auro cascading over his body like a reverse waterfall. He continued to growl as he focused, the gravity around him appearing to lessen as he began summoning his spirit beast. "I don't need a weapon to beat you both!" He snarled as spit flew from his mouth, landing on his chin. It wasn't long before his great ape spirit beast was summoned in front of him, its large protruding teeth as intimidating as Arnold might expect. Its colour and size were not natural for a spirit beast. The ape stood taller and larger than what an ape should be. Its colour matched the negative energy Valin was displaying, its fur appearing dark blue, almost black like the inside of its chest glowing a strange turquoise colour. The ape didn't hang around and it threw itself at Kaliska, who raised her spear on its side to defend herself. The ape took hold of it before roaring at Kaliska and bending the spear downwards. She tried in vain to fight against this, but the great ape was far stronger than anything she could match. It didn't take long before her spear snapped clean in half, the ape forcing it to splinter in two like a fickle matchstick.

The ape flung the splintered weapon to the floor and threw its forearm at Kaliska, slamming into her chest. As she lost her balance, the ape grabbed her and pressed her into the ground before standing over her, beating its chest with a primal rage. Arnold rushed forward to help her, but Valin was in his space. He moved far quicker than he had previously, giving Arnold little chance to react. He forced Arnold into the wall behind him, the cheers and jeers directly above him spurring on the onslaught. Valin gritted his teeth tightly as he pressed his arm against Arnold's neck whilst moving his free hand to Arnold's wrist to prevent him striking with his machuahuitl. Arnold slammed his fist into the side of Valin's head repeatedly, but his grip did not waver. As Arnold lost focus, he felt the energy he was summoning engulf him against his will. His body instantly started to spasm as he lost control of the weapon that he was spirit wielding.

Valin grinned before stepping backwards, letting Arnold crumple to the ground, convulsing violently as the spirit energy coursed around every part of him. Arnold felt powerless and in desperate need of regaining control. The pain was unbearable and something Arnold had not missed. Ahead of him, Kaliska lay sprawled out, the ape still beating its chest. It brought its fists up into the air, ready to bring them down on her, waiting for the command to end her.

Arnold fought against the energy with every ounce of strength that he could muster, knowing he needed to get up. He needed to regain control so he could help the leader of the Almec; she was completely defenceless against the spirit beast. He pushed back against the energy, accepting the pain, working with it. His arms and legs burned, a deep pain searing into his bones as he crawled to his knees, pushing his closed fists into the dirt as he tried to push himself upward.

"You have the best seat in the house to watch this," Valin teased, stepping behind Arnold and placing him in a headlock.

Arnold struggled against him, but Valin was too strong, forcing him to watch as the ape brought down its fists against Kaliska.

"No!" Marrok cried out, drowning out the noise of almost everyone who stood spectating.

Blood splattered from Kaliska's mouth as the ape beat its fists into her chest, Arnold heard the crunch of her ribs. The ape raised its fists once more as it readied for another blow.

Arnold continued to struggle, unable to escape Valin's grasp. He felt useless in his quest to save her. There was no way that Kaliska could survive another blow.

"Safe to say I have won this. I have bested the leader of the Almec and the famous Arnold Ethon. It hasn't been that difficult." He goaded.

"Please don't do this!" Arnold pleaded as he tried to push back once more, but Valin continued to pin him into place.

"End her," He commanded, mercilessly.

The ape roared, ready to strike down the fatal blow. At this moment, a distorted gateway opened to the side of Kaliska, catching the attention of the ape, who was distracted by the energy. Levent stepped through the gateway he had created. His powerful frame covered in the bone mail that the Almec wore, a lion's mane cast around his head. He took barely a second to take in the situation before slamming his fist into the side of the ape, pulling its attention away from the injured Kaliska.

"You can't do this; you can't step into this arena." Valin roared. His grip loosening ever so slightly as his focus was shifted.

Levent jumped onto the back of the ape and wrapped his arms around its head, holding on for life as the ape thrashed around.

The struggle continued with Levent looking as though he was riding on a wild bull; the ape doing everything it could to dislodge him. Levent held firm, gripping his arms as tightly as he could. He reached one of his hands down to his side and removed something from his waistband. Levent raised it high to reveal his dagger made of ivory and ebony. He plunged the dagger deep into the ape's side, who let out a deafening cry of pain. It swung its arm back at Levent, catching him in the head, but he held on. He pulled the dagger out before plunging it back into the side of the spirit beast for a second time. It continued to thrash about lunging at Levent once more, catching him over

215

and over, each time the power in its fist lessening. The ape fell forward; it dissipating back to Valin as his body absorbed the spirit once more.

"NOOO!" Valin cried, "This cannot be!" He roared, "He has broken the laws of the flower war. This man needs to be executed."

Taking his opportunity, Arnold flung his head back at Valin, catching him square in the chin. The crunch was deeply satisfying and Arnold rolled forwards before turning to face his enemy. Arnold did not know how Levent had managed this, but the fact he was wearing armour told Arnold that he had planned this. His intention was always to be here.

Valin stood opposite, blood pouring down from his broken nose, his auro slowly fading as his connection to his spirit beast slowly ended. He dropped to his knees in a weakened state. Arnold didn't hesitate and ran at Valin before throwing himself into a drop kick at him. Valin was no match for the blow and crumpled to the ground, unconscious and beaten.

The disapproval was apparent from above as the members of the Calmecac began heckling, and for a moment Arnold thought they might spill down the sides to fight and avenge their fallen champion.

Their shouts and cries were soon drowned out by a noise that shook Arnold to the core. It was a deafening roar, like nothing he had ever heard. Looking to his side, he saw Levent searching the skies, a panicked expression etched into his face. It was something Arnold had never seen from him, he knew there was only one thing of this earth that filled Levent with fear. An enormous shadow crept over the arena like a wave, fast and unrelenting.

The dragon had been summoned.

Arnold had only come across this beast when in his eagle form in the spirit world. He braced himself for what was to come, but the shadow of the dragon passed over them.

The dragon was heading to the other side of the arena and straight for the Elder council.

Chapter 24

It was chaos. The arena battle had not gone the way Arnold had imagined. Arnold had defeated Valin thanks to the intervention of Levent, but how was he able to enter the arena? Arnold was grateful, as it had saved Kaliska's life but he did not know what this would mean for the flower war.

The other warriors of the Calmecac spilled down the sides of the arena, unable to jump down the same as Valin, giving Arnold and Levent time to prepare.

The dragon's roar echoed on the far side as it made its way towards the Elder council. A mixture of aggressive shouts and cries rang out as the dragon reached them.

"What now?" Arnold asked, picking up his machuahuitl and readying himself to summon his spirit blade.

"Whatever it takes to survive, boy," Levent looked down at Kaliska longingly. There was a moment's pause as if Levent was desperate to say something but unable to all the same.

"Mum!," Marrok cried as he slid to a stop, reaching them and dropped to Kaliska's side to check her over. Her chest was moving, albeit slowly. She was badly injured but she was going to be ok. "I don't care about what you have done in the past, you saved her life. Thank you."

Levent simply nodded. He looked uncomfortable and unsure

of what to say.

"We can talk later, for now we have these to deal with," Arnold was referring to the twenty strong group of Calmecac that were reaching the bottom of the arena, their battle cries ringing out.

"Do what you need to," Kaliska mustered a few words through pained breaths. "Protect our ways Marrok."

Marrok stood tall, pulling his white wolf's pelt over the top of his head, his orange auro glowing around him. He summoned his wolf, which began howling as soon as its feet planted in this world, ready for battle. The noise of other spirit beasts soon echoed inside the arena as the other members of the Almec and their spirit beasts arrived to aid Kaliska and fend off the Calmecac.

Deers, hyenas, bears of different varieties all charged forward ahead of Arnold, Levent and Marrok, the white wolf leading the pack. Their numbers were fewer than the Calmecac, but their own warriors looked ready for the fight. Arnold noticed the yellow trail of George's fox and spun to see her firing towards them. She also wore bone mail and the pelt of a fox over her shoulders, the Almec having initiated her while Arnold had been training.

The Calmecac began summoning their spirit beasts in response. Arnold could see an orangutan, a bull, an alligator, an elephant. All of them distinct with the negative energy being used to summon them. Whatever Arnold's Grandma had done to Valin, she had also done with these. A wall of beasts smashed into each other, a spectacle that Arnold thought unimaginable unfolding right before him. Spirit beasts began biting, scratching, hitting each other venomously as they attempted to best one another. The elephant picked up a boulder with its trunk and launched it into the fray like a pebble.

It bounced off the ground, taking out two of the Almec's beasts. A man and a woman fell to the ground as they grappled with their spirit beast being injured.

Arnold, Marrok and Levent led the line of the Almec charging towards the battle with the others following behind. Levent was built more powerfully than them and such was faster than both. He charged just ahead of them with his dagger out stretched roaring his own battle cry that would have matched the lions that were once bound to his blade. The battle lines soon became a blur of man, woman and beast as the warring factions met in combat.

Levent was first to enter, disappearing in to the dust of of the fight before leaping upwards and slamming his blade into the side of the elephant's leg, causing it to buckle and fall.

Arnold entered the battle lines, the muffled sounds of different spirit beasts fighting engulfed him. The noise was incredible; the power being emitted was immense. Arnold felt as though he was in the centre of a tornado as the beasts flew around him, aggressively tearing chunks out of one another.

An axe drew down on him and Arnold knew that the warriors of the Calmecac had arrived. The sharpened blade barely missing him. He didn't have the energy to summon his blade, but he gripped the hilt tightly and wrapped it around the face of the attacker, rendering him unconscious. Then he slammed it into another and another until a flailing Gregor stopped his momentum. Gregor grinned, charged by the battle and swung a fist at Arnold, swatting him to the floor as if he was a fly. Arnold couldn't spirit walk here. There were too many people and spirit beasts summoned. Before he could jump to his feet, Gregor slammed his boot into his side, sending him rolling. He only stopped when he smashed into the side of a spirit beast glowing with negative energy. The alligator swung its head at Arnold and bit down like a vice, Arnold only just managing to move out of the way before a polar bear slammed its paws into the head of the alligator, forcing its gaping jaws to stay shut. With no time to think, Arnold was dodging the attack of an orangutan which had bundled towards him, far faster than what Arnold would have expected. Its arms were long and unpredictable and the power of the blow would have caused a great deal of damage had it connected. Arnold wrapped the hilt of his blade into the head of the orangutan, stunning it momentarily. It bought him the time he needed as a deer came charging in, using its tremendous antlers like a pike as it rammed into the orangutan.

Arnold stood panting, the battle unfolding around him; he did not know how this was going to end. Warriors fighting from either faction, weapons drawn. People laying on the ground injured, unconscious or even worse. He could not see Marrok or George and could only hope that they were ok. Never in a million years would Arnold of believed something like this could happen in today's society. The numbers were thinning as the injured and unconscious piled up on the floor. It looked to Arnold that there were more Almec than Calmecac standing, boosting Arnold's hopes that they may just do this, they may just survive this.

"Night Sun!" a woman shouted over the battlefield. It wasn't a cheer as Arnold expected from the Almec who considered Otto as a deity, it was a warning. They knew he was under the control of another.

Arnold's blood ran cold as the shrill roar of Otto greeted them, his teeth bared, snarling like a feral beast. He had shifted into the were jaguar, his skin lined with golden fur, his body decorated in the spots of a jaguar. He ran on all fours before leaping onto the woman that had cried out. Two more Almec warriors dived in to rescue her with Otto, flinging them around like a dog with a toy in its mouth. One of them fell to the floor, clutching his leg as blood spilled from him.

"Otto no!" George was closest and flew into him, her fox jumping and landing on one of his arms before sinking its teeth into him.

Otto flung his arm around wildly as George's fox hung on for dear life, its teeth deeply embedded, unshifting and unrelenting despite the clear size and power difference. George reached Otto and gripped the shaft of her staff tightly and wrapped this around Otto's head. It bounced off him and seemed to only anger Otto further as he roared in George's face. She was not intimidated by him in his feral form.

"Otto, you need to listen." She tried to reason with him, but it was fruitless. Otto backhanded her across the face, sending her to the floor before grabbing hold of her fox with the same hand. The fox yelped as he buried his claws into it and gripped it tightly. Otto flung the fox like it weighed nothing toward George, who winced as her fox clattered into her.

"George!" Marrok came charging in, his white wolf standing off against Otto whilst he checked over George, helping her to her feet. Her fox was injured and limping but it was still ready for the fight. Otto roared once more, but the two of them were unmoving.

"Otto, you are in there! We know you are in there. Remember, we trained for this!" Their spirit beasts charged forwards the fox latching onto one arm, the white wolf on the other. Otto shrieked as he waved his arms in an infuriated attempt to remove them from him, but they continued to stand firm.

222

"Otto, listen to me!" George pleaded. "Listen to my voice!"

He roared again and began walking towards her, dragging his injured arms and their spirit beasts with ease as he marched towards her. His head was twitching like he was shaking off his own thoughts, his eyes and body surrounded by his bright green auro.

"Listen to her Otto!" Marrok pleaded, "Listen to her!"

He moved forward to protect George and Otto flung his jaws at him and attempted to bite down. George rammed her staff in between his mouth as he bit down. He started gnawing at it as he attempted to push through and get to them both. All the while getting more and more feral, the more frustrated that he got.

Sensing an opportunity, Arnold darted forwards towards the three of them to help in any way he could. Otto was distracted by trying to get to George and didn't see Arnold arriving in his periphery. Arnold wrapped his arms around the arm that had George's fox latched on to and pulled him back slightly. Otto went to swing the arm with Marrok's wolf but found that it was unmoving. Levent had taken hold to pin him into place.

Otto continued to fight against them, but Arnold stood firm, gripping tightly against Otto's powerful arm, desperate for him not to hurt their friends. Levent was just as unrelenting but did not seem to struggle the same as Arnold. The two of them pulled his arms back to force some distance between Otto and George. Otto was far more powerful than Arnold had remembered, but last time he had faced him in this form he had used the coal mines to his advantage.

"Marrok, take hold of my staff." George asked.

Marrok grabbed hold of the staff as commanded and stood firmly as Otto continued to bite through it. The staff continued to match the glow of George's auro even though she no longer held it as she ducked underneath and towards Otto.

"George! what are you doing?!" Arnold struggled to form his words as he panicked that George was left unguarded and in Otto's striking range. She planted her hands against his chest, her auro pulsating against him. "Listen to my voice, we trained for this." She repeated. Arnold stopped biting against the staff and appeared to calm before biting down once more snapping back into his feral beast mode.

"Listen to me!" She pressed her hand's even harder against him as her energy grew and continued to pulsate against him. Arnold noticed his arms were less tense than they had been.

"It's working, George!" Arnold explained. "Whatever you are doing, it is working!"

"Now!" George commanded and Marrok stepped backwards, removing her staff from Otto's snapping jaws.

"What are you doing!" Arnold cried out. George was in immediate danger now as she stood vulnerable in front of Otto. Otto fell to his knees, halving his towering frame in an instance. George ran her hands up his chest until she had a hand on each side of his head, her auro continuing to pulsate into him. She grimaced at the amount of energy that she was channeling.

"Come on Otto, you can do this!" she growled through gritted teeth.

Otto tried to shake his head, to shake her off him, but George was determined and would not break her connection. There was another pull against Arnold and Levent, but they held firm as they stopped him from striking.

Otto was in a battle with himself. His head began twitching violently, his arms started jerking. George continued to use her auro to help him.

His eyes snapped out of its deep green glow, his auro fading. His tension in his arms giving up as he fell forward towards George. Marrok grabbed hold of her and pulled her out of the way. She nearly collapsed because of the amount of energy she had used. Otto fell forwards like a tree that had been felled and face planted into the ground, shifting out of his were jaguar form.

George dropped next to him, as did Marrok, both their spirit beasts forming a healing field around him. The yellow and orange auro's of Marrok and George blended perfectly as their spirit beast soothed Otto's injuries from the fight.

Another tremendous roar rang out from the top of the arena. Flashing lights of differing colours were filling the sky where the Elder council stood, but Arnold couldn't see anyone. The roar was clearly from the dragon and it wasn't long before Arnold caught a glimpse of it as it flew up high once again. Its silhouette cast in front of the sun as it surveyed its victims below. It dived towards them, disappearing out of sight again, Arnold knew he needed to help. He felt heavily fatigued, the battle was still ongoing, but the Almec were in control.

"Go help them," George told Arnold, "They are your people and they need your help."

"Go, we will be fine here." Marrok followed up.

Levent stared in the dragon's direction before giving Arnold a nod. He turned and ran into the remaining Calmecac warriors and their spirit beasts to continue the good fight.

Arnold set off across the arena once more, his legs burning, his body aching. He needed to get to the top of the arena as soon as possible; Arnold had an idea, but he had never tried it before and so did not know if it would work. He glowed as he summoned his spirit beast, his auro energising him and soothing his aching body. Either that or it was the adrenaline which was coursing through him. His eagle shrieked as he summoned it and it flew ahead of him before swooping high up and in a loop before bearing down behind Arnold. Running as fast as he could, Arnold sprang up into the air and his eagle grabbed hold of the back of his armour, peeling him upwards higher and higher.

The feeling was incredible. Arnold felt weightless and terrified at the same time. He did not know if their momentum would remain or if he would drop down and severely injure himself.

Arnold didn't fall; he kept rising and rising his connection to his spirit beast, feeling stronger than ever before. The two of them continued to soar until they flew out of the top of the arena. His armour felt as if it was connected to his skin. He could feel the air against the feathers that were fixed into the body of it. They vibrated intensely, but the feeling was soothing. If they weren't in the middle of a battle, he wished he could really push this skill to its limits with his eagle. As they exited the arena, a sense of euphoria was suddenly lost at the massacre before him. Bodies were strewn, bodies contorted into unnatural positions. Arnold was unsure who was dead and who was severely injured, but it didn't seem like anyone was getting off lightly. There were only two Elders remaining. It didn't take Arnold long to recognise who they were. Mr Whittaker and Miss Stone, his own Elder and the Grand Elder stood side by side fending off the dragon as best as they could. Their robes were torn, and they were battle weary. Mr Whittaker's face was charred. He looked as if he could barely stand, his right leg at a strange angle as if he wasn't able to bare weight on it. Miss Stone had her swan spirit beast summoned as Mr Whittaker's tiger prowled in front of them both as it tried to protect them.

The dragon had its feet planted on the ground, striking its scaled neck towards them as it tried to destroy the remaining members of the Elder council. Miss Stone's swan was flapping its wings in vain to deter the dragon but it took hold of one of its wings and dragged the powerless beast into the air and began violently shaking it around. Miss Stone dropped to her knees, weakened by the dragon's onslaught against her spirit beast, sharing one another's pain.

Arnold swooped low towards the dragon, tucking his arms in as the two of them dove towards the most powerful spirit beast to walk this earth. They flew past its head, distracting the dragon. It tossed the swan to one side before roaring violently at Arnold and his eagle. Memories of the beast chasing him in the spirit world flooded his mind, the fear of the dragon biting down on him more real than ever. They remained in the sky as the dragon took flight after them, wanting to end them both as much as the Elder council evidently.

What now? Arnold thought. He didn't have a plan. He simply wanted to protect Mr Whittaker and Miss Stone from the peril they were facing. He could feel the beast bearing towards him. Arnold tried to glance behind him but could only catch glimpses of the dragon's wings as it gave chase at a frightening pace. Arnold continued to duck dip and dive around the sky, dodging the dragon as it snapped at him. Each time it was getting closer and closer, Arnold knew he had little time. His eagle swooped up even higher into the air, the oxygen getting dangerously thin for Arnold. Their minds connected, the eagle turned, allowing Arnold to see the dragon in full form and dangerously close, its scales glistened in the sun as though they were metal. Its teeth bared, sharper and jagged, ready to tear him apart. The eagle let go of Arnold, who plummeted back down towards the dragon as it flew up towards him. He reached for his machuahuitl and focused his energy with every ounce of strength remaining. Surviving this was not the priority it was taking out this beast that was most important. His machuahuitl flickered, his auro charging the raw energy from the spirit world. Arnold pushed even harder and with another flicker, the machuahuitl was summoned just as the dragon reached him, its jaws wide apart and ready to finish him. Arnold turned, his velocity changing, meaning he was able to dodge the strike that would have ended him. Grabbing hold of the machuahuitl with both hands, he slammed the weapon into one of the dragon's wings and held on tightly. The blade cut through the wing like a knife to the sail of a ship; the dragon growled in pain as Arnold dragged the blade downwards until there was nothing left for the blade to rip through. Arnold spun wildly, plummeting to the ground, the world spinning around him just like when he shifted to the spirit world. There was no doubt in his mind that whichever world he was in when he hit the ground he would be met with nothingness, a darkness as he accepted his death.

He wasn't done yet though, and he fought against the turbulence of the air to regain his composure. He was sure his feathered armour should be able to assist him. He spun again, this time slower, and used the air pressure to balance himself out like a skydiver diving from a plane.

The ground was fast approaching, faster than Arnold would care to greet it, and he braced himself for the impact. He felt talons forced into his back and grimaced in pain as it pierced his armour. It was not the dragon that had grabbed him; it was his eagle. The eagle flapped its wings as fast and hard as it could as it attempted to slow the two of them down as they hurtled to the green field below them at incredible speed. It didn't take long for them to meet the grass, and the two of them bounced off the dirt like a pebble skimming water. Arnold's body bouncing violently until he eventually came to a stop. His eagle vanished instantaneously as it dissipated into him. It's injury from the fall too great. Arnold was still breathing, but he was in agony and he could feel his auro fading around him. He had nothing left to give, no energy left to fight with. He looked to the sky for the dragon in time to see it crash into the ground, unable to fly because of Arnold cutting through its wing. It roared loudly once more as it crashed down, engulfed by a dust cloud.

"Ethon!" He heard Mr Whittaker call out, but he didn't know where from or how far he was. Arnold knew he wasn't as close to him as the figure that moved to stand over him like a creeping shadow.

"Hello grandson!" The voice hissed. His Grandma took hold of him and dragged him to his feet. She was furious. A rage etched into her face that blemished her usual soft features. Her strength was greater than Arnold had imagined her to have as she pulled him close to her. "Persistent aren't you!" She growled. "You just had to save them, didn't you, couldn't you see how close you were to being free, for me having revenge."

Arnold spluttered, finding it hard not only to form words but to breathe. He was winded from the fall, however he still tried his hardest to respond. "This isn't the way" He stood firm, as firm as he could. If his Grandma was not gripping him by his arms he would collapse into a heap on the floor.

She pulled him closer. "I have no problem killing you, you have gotten in my way. You should never have made it this far.

Even ending your friend hasn't stopped you!" She goaded. "And what for? To see me finish what they started, they all deserve to die for what they have done to me."

"This was never about taking power, was it?" Arnold pointed out. "It was always about killing the Elders who you blame for being trapped in the spirit world."

"There we go," she smiled. "Don't you see Arnold? This has always been about revenge. We are not interested in anything else. By triggering the flower war, I knew that every single member of the council would be here. I knew that the Almec, who have been a constant thorn in my side for years, would be here too. It was simply too good of an opportunity to pass up on, kill all my enemies at once."

"Then what?"

His Grandma smiled a sinister smile, "Why does there always have to be a what next? Revenge is all I have ever wanted for the last fourty years! I do not care who gets injured along the way." She looked over Arnold's bloody and bruised body "Something you have had to learn the hard way. Like your friend," she sneered.

Arnold saw red at her, how dare she speak of Everett's death like it meant nothing. He flung his head forward, using the beak of his helmet to drag down her snarling face causing a large gash.

She screamed in pain and let go of Arnold, who crumpled to the floor like a sack of potatoes. He tried to push himself up, but he couldn't. He could see his Grandma holding her hand to her face, blood spilling through her enclosed fingers.

"I've had enough of your insolence, it's time to end this!" she roared as she pulled her own twisted dagger from her side and moved to plunge it into Arnold.

"Now, now mother," Levent appeared and grabbed hold of her arm, stopping her blade inches before it pierced Arnold's chest.

"What are you doing?" She furiously spat.

"Something I have planned for a long time!" He snarled back, his own fury creeping into his face.

"You can't kill us!" she glowered as she turned to smile.

"Levent look out!" Arnold warned.

The dragon hurtled towards them, badly injured but very much still alive. Levent spun and removed his ivory blade from its holster and rammed this into the dragon's chest as hard as he could. He gripped it tightly and held firm. The blade glowed an orange colour, as its powers activated.

"No, no!" His Grandma cried as she realised what was happening.

Levent's blade absorbed the dragon spirit beast as it bound itself to it, stealing its power from its host.

The dragon slowly disappeared into nothing, the blade glowing brightly in Levent's hand as he sought to control the power that he now held.

"What have you done!" His Grandma cried as she stretched out a newly wrinkled hand to her son. Her body was aging at an incredible rate. The last fourty years of time came flowing through her and her body became frail and weak. Her connection to her spirit beast severed. She had no energy to draw upon. She fell face first, wheezing through her aged lungs until she rasped her last breath.

Dragging himself to sit up, Arnold faced Levent. "You planned this all along, didn't you? You always wanted to wield the power of that dragon. It's what you wanted to do with me when you thought I had a dragon spirit beast."

"It's not what you think, Arnold," Levent explained.

"What is it then?" Arnold cried, confused about what Levent's intentions were.

"Redemption." He spoke before stretching out his hand and summoning a distorted gateway to the spirit world. "This spirit beast is too powerful. People will always seek it. People will always search for it. It needs to remain in the spirit world. That way it cannot corrupt anyone else, it needs to be hidden."

"What if someone can get through? What if someone is able to find it! What then?!" Arnold asked.

"I know more than anyone what this creature is capable of. Remember, I bear the scars of it. I have no intention of drawing on its power. I will be there to stop it falling into the hands of another." Levent moved to the portal before stepping through to the other side, the portal vanishing behind him, the last bit of pulsating energy eventually fading away.

Arnold was alone, but he could hear the calls of his allies as they made their way to help him. He fell onto his back and grimaced at the pain he was feeling.

The battle was over; they had won, against all the odds.

Chapter 26

Chapter 25

Arnold sat in the back of an ambulance. He had been given the once over and his arm had been placed into a temporary sling. He had removed his helmet, his face was covered in cuts and bruises, his right eye swollen shut. His body ached like never before. His bones felt as though they may crumble to dust, his muscles battered and bruised. The media had caught wind of what had happened and were descending on the area like unwanted wasps at a picnic. Doyen's from the surrounding areas were doing a good job of keeping them at bay whilst the paramedics set to work on saving those who still had life in them.

George, Marrok and Otto made their way towards Arnold, who was busy surveying the situation. They all looked battle weary. George and Marrok's armour was broken and their faces decorated with bruises. Otto's clothes were in tatters from his transition into the were jaguar, he looked pale and struggled to walk as he approached. George's eyes caught Arnold's, and she cast him a delicate smile as they approached him.

"How are you feeling?" She asked him.

"Like I have been run over by a truck." Arnold winced as he attempted to stand up.

"George, how were you able to help Otto?" Arnold didn't

beat around the bush, having seen George in action on the battlefield.

"Kaliska taught me." She started. "Kaliska always believed that Otto's connection to the blade could be broken. She has been helping me control my abilities using techniques that her Dad had shown her. He was the shaman. I guess I kind of am now."

Arnold reached to his side and took hold of something. He brought it up to pass to Otto. "Well, I guess there is only one way of knowing," He passed the dagger towards him. He had removed it from his Grandma following the fight. "If you can hold it, then the connection is broken. You couldn't hold it before, could you?"

Tentatively, Otto outstretched his hand and received the dagger, breathing a sigh of relief as it landed in his palm. He gripped it tightly, struggling for words. A lump gathered in his throat, his eyes welling up with tears. "It was too much to ask anyone to wield this. It wasn't Everett's fault."

The four of them stood in silence for a moment as they thought about their fallen friend. Otto looked to the skies. "I'm going to miss you Ev,"

"We all are." George's eyes were wet with tears too, her emotions catching up with her now the dust had settled.

Arnold wrapped his better arm around her, Marrok doing the same, then Otto hugging all of them together. They stayed in this moment for a while as they comforted each other, all of them in tears as they thought about Everett.

Miss Stone hobbled over to them, interrupting the moment. "I am sorry to interrupt. I just needed to say thank you to you. To all of you. I saw what you did out there. You all fought with bravery and honour. Arnold, I will be eternally grateful for you saving myself and Mr Whittaker and the other members of the Elder council."

"How many made it?" Arnold pressed, knowing how bleak it had looked when he first arrived.

"Not everyone, but there would have been more fatalities had you not intervened when you did." Miss Stone explained. "You put your life on the line to protect us all."

"Where's Mr Whittaker?" Arnold asked, wanting to know if he was ok.

"He's on his way to the hospital, he has a pretty deep gash down his leg that needs tending to."

"What about the flower war?" Marrok interrupted, "What do we do about this complete mess?"

"I believe Levent could enter the fight because of his blood tie to you, Arnold. I also saw enough to see that Valin had already been bested during the battle. Kaliska was not unconscious. This means the battle is undecided.' Miss Stone explained, 'Perhaps this is for the best." She deduced; she didn't look too sure herself on what the outcome of the flower war should be.

"That doesn't feel right," Arnold couldn't keep quiet, "That only benefits us. Things need to change."

"The overall champion decides who keeps control, the losing factions submitting to their will." She pointed out.

"Yes, but these were written millennia ago, surely we need to change this." Arnold argued.

"I agree, some rules could do with tweaking, but others such as the outcome are bound by deep, powerful magic and we must adhere to them."

"Maybe I can help," a voice called out from behind Miss Stone.

"Mum!" Marrok shot towards her and wrapped his arms around her. Her body was bound tightly with a bandage, and she winced as Marrok squeezed her tightly.

"You all fought bravely," Kaliska echoed Miss Stone's sentiments. "But I agree with Arnold that change is needed. The Almec needs a voice, the Calmecac needs a voice. That way there need be no further flower wars. As I believe, the champion would have the power to implement this."

"There is no champion Kaliska, not unless you and Arnold wish to fight right now." Miss stone suggested. She looked irritated at the thought of another battle.

"I am done with fighting and as much as I do not trust the Chichen, I do trust you Arnold." Kaliska bowed her head and dropped to one knee, albeit gingerly. "Arnold Ethon, I yield." Kaliska looked up to smile at Arnold before being helped back to her feet by Arnold. "I believe we have our champion." she finished.

Miss Stone looked shocked at what she had just witnessed, her face becoming paler. She stuttered for her words, "I believe you are right, by the laws of the flower war you have yielded, thus declaring our champion Arnold."

Arnold did not know what was happening. Suddenly he had been declared champion, and he felt as though suddenly he had the world on his shoulders. All eyes were on him at once.

"I agree with Kaliska, the balance of power needs to be shared. A new system, one where all three factions have a voice. Where no one faction rules over the others. Surely we can only get stronger by this." Arnold declared.

"Very well, our champion has spoken. It will be met with some resistance, but the magic that surrounds the flower war binds us. It won't happen straight away but I suggest as the dust settles we sit down and plan how this is going to work." Miss Stone turned to leave. She looked shell-shocked at Arnold's decision but was bound to honour it all the same.

"Arnold, the Calmecac bloodline runs through you, through your Grandma. There is an opportunity for you to bring balance to them. Something that I think you should think about seriously as champion."

"Let's see what we can do." Arnold responded. "We need to get this right."

"Thank you Arnold, for all that you have done. For all of us." Kaliska turned to leave to check on the injured members of the Almec.

"You did it Arnold, you bloody did it." Otto hugged Arnold so tightly with pride that Arnold thought his head might pop. "Arnold Ethon, supreme leader!" He looked puzzled by the others' quizzical expressions at the title he had just thought up.

"Bit sinister that Otto, but let's see what we can do." Arnold smiled at his friends, proud of what they had achieved. There was a long way to go, but the flower war was over. His Grandma stopped and the dragon spirit beast that had corrupted her sealed away in the spirit world. All that needed to happen now was for the Chichen, Almec and Calmecac to work together. If everyone could work together on a dark day like today, then tomorrow looked that little bit brighter.

Epilogue

Sitting on one of the chairs in the lock up Arnold sat tentatively a dusted journal sat on his lap. There was so much Arnold had learned about his Grandad from this journal, there was just one more entry that was left to read. It was something that Arnold had put off for so long, part of him wanted to read his Grandad's thoughts, part of him not wanting to finish reading his words.

Looking over the leather bound journal Arnold ran his fingers over the dust that settled on the cover before opening it and moving to the back of the book.

Exhaling he fixed his eyes on the words that decorated the page.

5th July 2015

I am lost, the things that I have done, the things that I have witnessed. I write these words as I am due to retire as the Elder of Lancashire. To those within the Chichen they see a man committed to our ways, it is only myself who knows what goes on in my mind. The Chichen collect or more accurately apprehend or better still steal artefacts from others all over the world. For years I have been part of this system that has sworn to protect others by not allowing these powerful artefacts to fall into the wrong hands. I believed this cause

I believed in what we did for so long, for most of the time that I have served the Chichen. My thoughts changed the day that we ambushed a wedding, the day that we took from the Almec.

It never sat well with me what happened that day which is why I reached out afterwards. Why I spent so may years searching for them, to find a way to make amends. I was responsible for those with me that day, although their actions were in the name of the Chichen attacking those people was not a command that I gave. However as Elder I have to take responsibility for that, I have to make amends for what happened.

Over the years Kaliska has become a key ally and friend as she has taught me the ways of the Almec. Their views differ from the Chichen, somehow I need to find a way for their voices to be heard. Unknown to the Chichen, Kaliska and the Almec have helped me on numerous occasions. They are good people led by a strong leader. Kaliska has every right to be driven by vengeance, but she just wants a world where her people and her son can live in peace. They want to form an alliance with Chichen, not to overthrow it, despite what they did to her.

I am weary, I am tired and my time as Elder is coming to an end and thus my influence within the Chichen diminishes.

There is hope however in my grandson, Arnold. This is the reason why I have always written these journals, so my thoughts could pass on to the next generation. Arthur is strong minded and is climbing the ranks within the Chichen, he is not ready to hear my thoughts on this. I know that in time that both Arthur and Arnold will shape the world in more ways than are imaginable.

They have already shaped mine.

Hershel Ethon

Arnold didn't fight back the tears, he embraced them as raw emotion engulfed him. He knew that his Grandad would be

240

proud of everything that he had achieved, he knew he would be proud of the man that he had become.

A Final Word From The Author

Wow, what can I say. When I began writing Arnold Ethon And The Lions Of Tsavo I wanted to push myself to do something I had never done before, write a book. Here we are having finished the last book in this series. Three months after releasing my first book we were hit by the COVID pandemic and the world changed overnight. Determined I carried on writing and releasing my books, spurred on by readers who have come to love Arnold and his friends as much as I have loved writing about them. I want to take the opportunity to thank everyone who has supported me with my writing and you for taking the time to read my books. I cannot tell you the positive impact writing these books has had on my life.

At the time of finishing this book the world is looking pretty scary with the recent invasion of Ukraine. It is for this reason I would like anyone who finishes this series to focus on the last line of the story.

'If everyone could work together on a dark day like today, then tomorrow looked that little bit brighter.'

I wrote this before recent events happened, over a year ago in fact. For me these are the truest words I think I ever have or ever will write.

Thanks for all your support
A.P Beswick

About The Author

A.P Beswick loves telling stories and in between writing practicing as a Registered Mental Health Nurse. A.P has a passion for learning disabilities and has dedicated the last 13 years of his life to improving community services in this sector.

A.P hails from the funky little town known as Oswaldtwistle where he lives with his wife Sarah and their daughter Etta. A.P also has two more children Libbi and Connor with the three of them being the inspiration behind A.P Beswick Publications.

Join my newsletter HERE

Printed in Great Britain
by Amazon